THE British BASTARD

Other Books by Anna Durand

The Notorious Dr. MacT (A Hot Scots Prequel)
Dangerous in a Kilt (Hot Scots, Book One)
Wicked in a Kilt (Hot Scots, Book Two)
Scandalous in a Kilt (Hot Scots, Book Three)
The MacTaggart Brothers Trilogy (Hot Scots, Books 1-3)
Gift-Wrapped in a Kilt (Hot Scots, Book Four)
Notorious in a Kilt (Hot Scots, Book Five)
Insatiable in a Kilt (Hot Scots, Book Six)
Lethal in a Kilt (Hot Scots, Book Seven)
Irresistible in a Kilt (Hot Scots, Book Eight)
Devastating in a Kilt (Hot Scots, Book Nine)
Spellbound in a Kilt (Hot Scots, Book Ten)
Incendiary in a Kilt (Hot Scots, Book Twelve)
Lachlan in a Kilt (The Ballachulish Trilogy, Book One)
Aidan in a Kilt (The Ballachulish Trilogy, Book Two)
Rory in a Kilt (The Ballachulish Trilogy, Book Three)
Brit vs. Scot (A Hot Brits/Hot Scots/Au Naturel Crossover Book)
The American Wives Club (A Hot Brits/Hot Scots/Au Naturel Crossover Book)
One Hot Chance (Hot Brits, Book One)
One Hot Roomie (Hot Brits, Book Two)
One Hot Crush (Hot Brits, Book Three)
The Dixon Brothers Trilogy (Hot Brits, Books 1-3)
One Hot Escape (Hot Brits, Book Four)
One Hot Rumor (Hot Brits, Book Five)
One Hot Christmas (Hot Brits, Book Six)
One Hot Scandal (Hot Brits, Book Seven)
One Hot Deal (Hot Brits, Book Eight)
Natural Obsession (Au Naturel Nights, Book One)
Natural Passion (Au Naturel Trilogy, Book One)
Natural Impulse (Au Naturel Trilogy, Book Two)
Natural Satisfaction (Au Naturel Trilogy, Book Three)
Fired Up (standalone romance)
Echo Power (Echo Power Trilogy, Book One)
Echo Dominion (Echo Power Trilogy, Book Two)
Echo Unbound (Echo Power Trilogy, Book Three)
The Mortal Falls (Undercover Elementals, Book One)
The Mortal Fires (Undercover Elementals, Book Two)
The Mortal Tempest (Undercover Elementals, Book Three)
The Janusite Trilogy (Undercover Elementals, Books 1-3)
Obsidian Hunger (Undercover Elementals, Book Four)
Unbidden Hunger (Undercover Elementals, Book Five)
The Thirteenth Fae (Undercover Elementals, Book Six)
Echo Power (Echo Power Trilogy, Book One)
Echo Dominion (Echo Power Trilogy, Book Two)
Echo Unbound (Echo Power Trilogy, Book Three)
Passion Never Dies: The Complete Reborn Series

A Hot Scots Prequel

ANNA DURAND

JACOBSVILLE BOOKS · MARIETTA, OHIO

THE BRITISH BASTARD

ISBN: 979-8-9852412-3-5 (paperback)
ISBN: 979-8-9852412-4-2 (ebook)
ISBN: 979-8-9852412-5-9 (audiobook)

Manufactured in the United States.

Jacobsville Books
www.JacobsvilleBooks.com

Publisher's Cataloging-in-Publication Data
provided by Five Rainbows Cataloging Services

Names: Durand, Anna, author.
Title: The British bastard / Anna Durand.
Description: Marietta, OH : Jacobsville Books, 2021. | Series: Hot Scots prequel, bk. 2.
Identifiers: ISBN 979-8-9852412-3-5 (paperback) | ISBN 979-8-9852412-4-2 (ebook) | ISBN 979-8-9852412-5-9 (audiobook)
Subjects: LCSH: College teachers--Fiction. | Man-woman relationships--Fiction. | Scots--Fiction. | British--Fiction. | Romance fiction. | BISAC: FICTION / Romance / Contemporary. | FICTION / Romance / Romantic Comedy. | GSAFD: Love stories.
Classification: LCC PS3604.U724 B75 2021 (print) | LCC PS3604.U724 (ebook) | DDC 813/.6--dc23.

Chapter One

Alex

I lie here in this bed, in a posh hotel suite in a strange town, and wonder why I keep seducing women whose names I don't care to learn and who I never intend to see again. Oh, I know why. It's because I'm a bastard. I can't risk getting to know anyone too well, which means I will never allow myself to become embroiled in any sort of romantic relationship, whether I want that or not. My desires are irrelevant. So I roll onto my side and slap the hip of the anonymous American woman lying naked beside me. "Time for me to go, pet."

She pouts. "Stay a little longer, or even for the night. This was so much fun."

"Yes, but I'm tired of you now. Sorry, darling, it's time to say good night."

This woman has a fantastic body and an insatiable hunger for sex, but I do not want to fuck her again. She kept shouting, "I love your dick, I love your dick!" What a bloody stupid phrase to repeat over and over during sex. I realized the moment I saw her in the hotel bar that she has the IQ and temperament of a chihuahua, but I hadn't chosen her for my fling because I wanted to plumb the depths of her soul. I needed a good shag, that's all. I wish I could meet an intelligent, beautiful, sweet woman who arouses not only my lust, but also my curiosity. I can't search for a soul mate, though, if that sort of thing even exists. I cannot get involved with anyone. No girlfriends, no mates, no ties whatsoever. Only two people in all the world know the real me—not Dr. Alex Thorne, professor of archaeology, but the lost boy who still hides inside that persona.

"You're gorgeous," my bedmate purrs. "But why does a hot British guy live in New Mexico?"

"None of your business, pet." I slide off the bed and start reassembling my clothes. "You don't need to know anything about me, and vice versa."

She crawls across the bed toward me, apparently assuming I can't resist her naked body. She's wrong.

I pull my shoes on, check that my wallet is still inside my trouser pocket, and march out the door without glancing back. Why did I choose that woman for tonight's lover? Because I know I can never care for a pouting sex kitten like her. She's probably married to a geriatric multimillionaire. I walk at a brisk pace as I head for my car, which I'd parked two blocks from the hotel. Yes, I might also have hired a car for this occasion, strictly to make it harder for anyone to track me. Privacy matters to me, more so than for most people.

I return the car to the rental agency and drive my personal vehicle for the rest of the two-hour trip to my home.

Do I sleep well? No. But that's a frequent problem for me. I awaken in the morning feeling less than enthused about the day ahead, because classes begin this morning. I'm destined to spend the day lecturing to students who would rather be playing video games or shagging in their dorm rooms. As much as I look forward to my new job as an associate professor of archaeology and ancient history at Ballesteros University, I always feel a bit exposed whenever I need to speak in public. I'm not shy, but I have reasons for this anxiety. It's only a twinge, anyway. Hardly anything at all.

I go to my office to get situated, but once I've finished, I realize I still have thirty minutes before my first class begins. What should I do? Sit here in my office fiddling with pens and pencils? My gaze shifts to the window and the sunshine outside. Fresh air sounds good.

So I grab a book—the text I'll be teaching from today—and make my way to the quad and one of the benches I find there, under a tree that shades me from the heat of the sun. Sitting down, I lay the textbook on my lap and begin to browse the chapters. Yes, all right, maybe I should have read the text before today, but honestly, I know more about archaeology than the stuffed shirts who wrote this book. Still, I dutifully skim the pages. And I groan. I could've written a better book than this when I was a teenager.

Movement peripherally catches my attention, and I glance up.

A beautiful girl hovers a few yards away, clutching a spiral-bound notebook to her chest. A rucksack hangs over one shoulder, but it's not her academic paraphernalia that seizes my attention. She has the loveliest face I've ever seen, with blue eyes as pale as glacial ice and cinnamon hair that complements her creamy complexion. I love the faint pinkness of her cheeks, which seems natural rather than cosmetic. Her thick hair tumbles over her shoulders and nearly reaches her full breasts. I can't see those mounds, but I can imagine what they might look like.

She's a student. I should not be fantasizing about her naked body.

I can't help it. My lips curve up a touch, and like a moron, I wave at her. "Hello there."

The girl smiles shyly.

"You must be new here," I say. "You have that slightly dazed look about you."

She nods.

Her shyness makes me want to pull her into my arms and kiss her. Unlike the woman I'd shagged last night, this girl does not shamelessly flirt with me or devour my body with her gaze. She just stands there, seeming uncomfortable yet curious. She is a breath of fresh air, and I want to inhale every bit of her sweetness.

I close my book and shimmy sideways to make room. Then I pat the bench beside me. "Have a seat. Maybe I can help you with that confusion."

She bites her lip.

Can't stop myself. I grin at the adorable girl.

And she finally shambles over to the bench to sit down beside me.

I offer her my hand. "I'm Alex Thorne."

The girl slips her hand into mine. "Catriona MacTaggart. I just moved here from Scotland. To get my PhD."

"Ah, a grad student." I can't make myself release her hand because I love the feel of her soft, warm palm clasped to mine. "What department dent are you in?"

Catriona hesitates. "Archaeology."

Did she think I'd be disappointed by that fact? I can't resist moving my thumb over her skin in slow circles. "Me too. But I'm not your adviser, that I'm sure of. I'd remember being assigned a Scots student."

"No, you're not my adviser. I haven't met her yet."

"Just set foot on campus, have you?"

"Aye."

I smile again, enchanted by the angel beside me. "I do love the way Scots speak. Your accent is lovely."

"I like yours too."

Her eyes widen briefly, as if she thinks she's made an egregious error in etiquette. If she knew me, she wouldn't worry about rubbish like propriety. Not sure I want her to experience my world, though. She's perfect, just as she is.

And I am toxic.

"Thank you," I say in response to her statement. Then I tip my head to the side to study her and imagine what it would feel like to kiss her sensuous lips. "I hope we'll see each other again sometime. Even though I'm not your adviser, feel free to stop by my office anytime."

"I appreciate that." She pulls her hand free of mine and gets up. "I need to go, or I'll be late for my first meeting with my adviser."

"Good luck, Catriona."

She gives me another sweet little smile, then walks away.

But she glances back at me several times before she disappears from view.

That lass wants me. I want her too, but getting involved with any woman is too dangerous. Dating a student probably wouldn't violate the university's ethics rules, since Catriona is a graduate student. So I could ask her out, strictly to discover if we have as much chemistry as I think we do. No, I cannot do that. *Stay away from the bonnie Scots lass, you sodding arse.*

Being with me would stain her sweet soul.

My morning goes the way I'd thought. I attempt to force-feed education to students who can't stop chatting to each other. I resign myself to having only half the class, at most, listening to my lecture. At lunch, I grab food from the cafeteria and eat in my office with the door closed and locked. If students want to confer with me, they'll have to wait until another day. In the afternoon, I make my way to a different lecture hall to give another lesson, but this time, I have a room full of fourth-year students who seem more inclined to pay attention.

A miracle, for sure.

In the middle of my lecture about ancient Rome, I glance around the cavernous hall to make eye contact with some of the students. Most of them I can't see because they're in the back, too far away from me. I'm surprised I have a full house for this lecture. But I only consider that thought for half a second. Then my attention veers to a familiar face.

Catriona MacTaggart stands near the open door, at the top of the sloping floor.

Our gazes collide. I can't look away from her, and I realize I've stopped speaking. Even when I return to my lecture, I can't look away from Catriona, and she gazes right back at me as if she can't look away either. The lass who loves my accent seems entranced, but I don't think it's because of the subject matter. She has hypnotized me, and I know I will need to speak to her again, soon, if only to hear her lovely voice again.

No, I will not do that. Never again will I speak to her.

My resolve lasts only until the students vacate the hall. I see Catriona lingering by the open door as if she's waiting for me. I could exit via the other set of doors on the opposite side of the hall, but that would make me a bleeding coward. Walking past the Scots lass won't be difficult at all. If she tries to grab me, I will overpower her.

Oh, bloody hell. Now I'm afraid a woman will assault me because she's so desperately attracted to me. Even I'm not that arrogant.

I nod to Catriona as I pass her. She says nothing. But just as I turn to head down the corridor, I hear her voice.

"Dr. Thorne?"

I haltingly turn toward her and affect an air of casual interest. "Yes, Ms. MacTaggart?"

"Please call me Catriona." She squares her shoulders and lifts her chin. "You said I could come to your office anytime."

Oh, fuck. I'd also said I hoped I would see her again. When did I develop loose lips? Mine have always been tightly sealed. But if I tell her to go away… Nothing bad will happen. Yes, I should tell her to bugger off. Those aren't the words that come out of my mouth, though.

"My office is on the second floor," I tell her. "We can talk while we walk."

Catriona smiles. "Thank you, Dr. Thorne."

I start down the corridor with Catriona beside me, and she keeps smiling in the sweetest way.

Oh yes, I am doomed.

Chapter Two

Catriona

Alex Thorne is the most beautiful man I've ever seen, and I get a flutter in my tummy every time I see him. I've only seen him twice, but the fluttering happened on both occasions. He makes me feel like a teenage virgin, which inspires my mouth to say silly things and my body to behave like a shy schoolgirl. What must Alex think of me? I've acted like an eejit. Maybe he wears pheromone cologne so he can seduce lasses more easily.

As we walk up the stairs toward the second floor, I can't help noticing his body. He clearly has muscles under his dress shirt and trousers. Since I'd gazed into his eyes while we had our wee conversation on that bench in the quad, I know he has gorgeous brown eyes that seem almost the same shade as his hair. Whenever he smiles, a tingly sensation sweeps over my skin, and I suddenly can't piece together a single word. How could any woman stay coherent in his presence? Alex reminds me of a Michelangelo statue, the picture of masculine beauty and angelic grace.

I wonder if his, um, private parts resemble the statue of David.

Oh, for heaven's sake. I am a grown woman, not a bairn, and a PhD student too. It's time I stop gawping at Alex.

He leads me into his office and sits down behind the desk, then gestures for me to take one of the chairs in front of him. The sunlight streaming through the windows paints his features in shades of gold, accentuating his full lips. What would it feel like if he kissed me? I'd wager he knows how to kiss a woman, not like the lads back home who can't figure out what to do with their tongues.

I'm sure Alex knows exactly what to do with his tongue.

"Catriona?" he says. "Are you all right?"

"What? Oh, aye." Settling onto my chair, I set my rucksack on the floor and fold my hands on my lap. "This is a nice office."

Maybe if I'd tried harder, I could've said something even stupider.

"Thank you." His lips kink up at one corner. "I've never been complimented on my office before."

"Well, I, um—" *Haud yer wheesht, ye eejit.*

Alex relaxes against his chair and raises his brows. "What did you want to discuss with me?"

"I'm bothering you. Aren't I, Dr. Thorne?"

"Not at all. And please call me Alex." He gives me a wry smile. "Dr. Thorne sounds like the name of a Victorian arse."

"I think it's a sexy name." Why the bloody hell did I say that? Maybe I should ask him for a roll of tape so I can seal my stupid lips.

"Sexy?" he says while smiling even more. His eyes twinkle in the sunlight. "Well, that name is beginning to grow on me. But I'd still rather you called me Alex. All right?"

"Aye."

He studies me for a moment while gently rocking his chair. "You still haven't told me what I can do for you, Catriona. I'm not your adviser, so…"

I have no idea what I wanted him to do for me. All I thought about was how much I wanted to see him again. "You teach archaeology. That's what I'm studying in my PhD program, so I hoped you might have advice or suggestions."

"For what? Those would be questions for your adviser."

"Oh. Aye, of course."

He tips his head to the side, gazing at me with curiosity. "How long have been in America?"

"Eight days."

"No wonder you seem ill at ease here. Do you have any mates in this country?"

I shake my head. "Donnae know anyone. Well, except for you."

"And your adviser."

Does he keep mentioning that because he wants me to go away and leave him alone? Maybe I do feel a wee bit out of place here in another country, far from my home. But I cannae tell Alex that.

"I've been in America for a few years," he says. "So I can understand what you might be feeling right now. Perhaps I could be your adviser on how to acclimate to a new and very different environment. It might be more accurate to say we could be mates."

He wants to be my friend? My pulse accelerates, and that fluttery sensation returns. Aye, I want to be Alex's mate a bit too much.

"What do you say?" he asks. "Will you be my mate, Catriona?"

"Aye. That would be, um, lovely."

His mouth slides into a sexy grin. "Brilliant."

I pick up my rucksack. "You must have work to do, so I'll leave you to that."

"Yes, I do have lessons to plan. However, I'm free this evening." He eyes me up and down, and his tongue flicks out to moisten his lips. "Would you have dinner with me, Catriona? As a mate."

Will dinner with him be a platonic event? I'm not sure. My attraction to him could have influenced how I interpret his actions and words. Maybe he isn't attracted to me. He might only want to help a newcomer to this country.

But I need him to want me the way I want him.

"That would be lovely," I say. "Thank you, Alex."

"Where are you staying?"

"Graduate student housing. I have my own flat."

His lips twitch, though it's not quite a smile. "I know where that is. May I pick you up at eight?"

"Yes. I'll be ready."

"Excellent." He stands and escorts me to the open doorway. "I look forward to seeing you again, Catriona."

"I look forward to seeing you too, Alex."

As I walk down the corridor, I can't help glancing back. Alex is still standing on the threshold of his office, watching me. I wave to him, and he waves back. This time, though, I do not look back four more times. No, I restrain that impulse and keep moving at a brisk pace while I exit the building, cross the quad, and find my vehicle in the car park. I think Americans call it a parking lot. Tonight, Alex can help me get used to the way people in this country speak and teach me their idioms. I do know some of them from watching American television.

I shut the car door and sag into my seat. Cannae stop my lips from forming a smile or my body from tingling yet again. Alex Thorne wants to have dinner with me. Aye, with *me*.

Since I have no more classes today, I drive back to my flat in the graduate housing complex. I've just walked into the bedroom and kicked off my shoes when the phone on the bedside table rings. I snatch it up. "Hello?"

"Cat, how are you settling in?"

"Lachlan?"

"Aye, it's me. I asked how—"

"I'm settling in fine." Should I tell my oldest brother about Alex? No, not yet. We're just friends, anyway. "It's only my first day on campus, so ye donnae need to check up on me yet."

"Of course I do. My wee sister is on another continent, and you've been there for eight days."

"Ahmno 'wee,' and I can take care of myself."

"I know that." Lachlan pauses as someone in the background speaks, but I can't tell who it is or what that person says. "Rory wants to say hello."

Honestly, my brothers are so overprotective.

Rory comes on the line. "Are you sure you're all right, Cat? America is nothing like Scotland."

"How would you know? You've never been here."

"No, but Iain told me what it's like."

I can't help making a derisive noise. "He lived in this country for one year."

"Which means he has one year's more experience than you."

All I can do is sigh. "I'm fine, Rory. And I'm a grown woman who can take care of herself."

"Fair enough. Do you like it over there?"

At first, I felt homesick. But since I met Alex… Aye, things are looking up. "Yes, I do like it here. Satisfied, Rory?"

"We are your brothers. That means we have the right and the responsibility to check on you."

"Fine, aye, you do."

I chat to my brothers for a while, then we say goodbye. It must be the middle of the night in Scotland, yet my brothers rang me just to make sure I'm all right. Aye, I love them. And aye, I miss my family. But I don't regret moving to America.

For the next few hours, I debate what I should wear for my dinner with Alex. It's not a date. But I don't want to dress like a student. I want to present myself as a woman. How do I do that? Why do I want to do it? The how part is fairly simple, but I can't explain why I care if Alex views me as a woman instead of a student. Oh, aye, it's a mystery. That desire has nothing to do with how attracted I am to Alex.

I eventually decide on a pale-blue dress with a hem just above my knees and matching shoes. Then I realize I should really shave my legs, and after that, I spend twenty minutes putting on makeup and fixing my hair. I decide to leave my hair loose because I like the way it feels brushing against my bare shoulders. No, I don't care what Alex thinks of the way I'm dressed. I wanted to feel feminine for me, not for him.

Someone knocks on my door at precisely eight o'clock.

I rush to pull the door open and smile when I see Alex standing there.

"Are you ready?" he asks. "I've reserved a table at a restaurant that sounds quite nice."

"Yes, I'm ready."

He offers me his arm. "You look stunning, Catriona."

"Thank you." I hook my arm around his and take note of his charcoal suit and golden tan dress shirt that has two buttons undone. "You look very handsome yourself."

But he looks more than handsome. The color of his shirt complements the warm brown of his eyes, and the suit makes him look so dapper and sexy that I experience the strongest wave of tingly anticipation that I've ever felt in my life.

Alex leads me down the concrete steps and across the concrete walkway, guiding me straight to his car. It's a Mercedes convertible, though he hasn't rolled the top down. Is Alex rich? I didn't think associate professors made that much money. Not that I will ever ask him about that.

He opens the passenger door for me and offers me his hand as I climb into the car. Then he hurries to the driver's side and settles into his seat.

We glance at each other at the same time and smile at each other too. Gooseflesh pebbles my arms. I have never been this excited to spend time with any man, even one who only wants to be my mate.

As Alex drives the Mercedes down the streets of Ballesteros, I gaze at his profile and wonder what will happen next.

Chapter Three

Alex

Dinner with a student? I've lost my mind. The fact that she's a grad student and that I am not her adviser doesn't make me feel any less uncomfortable with what I've done. The university ethics code does not bar professors from dating students, and honestly, I never used to worry about that sort of thing. My conscience seems to have decided now is the right time to wake up from its long slumber.

Yes, all right, I want Catriona. As more than a mate. I want to strip her naked and do very unprofessional things to that body.

But I won't do it.

When we reach the restaurant, a waiter leads us to our table. It's a corner booth in a secluded area, just as I'd requested. I might not have ever visited this establishment before, but when I requested a table with a romantic atmosphere, the gent on the phone had assured me he would arrange that. I'm certain it helped that I offered him a large monetary inducement. Why I've gone to this much trouble, I can't explain. I shag women and don't ask for their names or give them mine. Yet with Catriona, I needed to…impress her.

It's bollocks. But here I am, placing a hand on her back as we wend our way through the tables to our booth.

Catriona slides into the semicircular booth first, then smiles at me.

I'm sure she expects me to sit right beside her, but I maintain an arm's length of distance instead. The waiter hands us menus and then leaves us alone. In this booth. Where no one else can see us. I've never taken a woman to a restaurant before, so this is new territory—and I haven't the slightest idea how to handle it.

The Scots lass pats the bench between us. "You can sit closer to me, Alex. I don't mind."

"Well, I, ah, don't want to crowd you." What a twat I've become since this morning. I don't want to crowd her? It's ridiculous.

Catriona smiles again. "It's all right. Please come closer. It's hard to talk to each other when you're so far away."

She makes it sound as if a continent separates us.

But I can't seem to control my own body, and I find myself sliding across the bench until I sit no more than a foot away from her. "Happy now?"

"Aye."

I flip open my menu and study my options while I take a sip of water.

Catriona leans in, her breasts brushing against my arm. "I see oysters on the menu. Have you ever eaten those?"

I choke on my water and barely avoid spewing it across the table. "What? No, I've never had those."

"Are you all right, Alex?"

She just asked if I want to eat an aphrodisiac, so no, I am not all right. Her nearness doesn't help matters. So I do what I'm best at—avoiding the truth by deflecting the question. "Tell me, Catriona, do you have any siblings?"

"Oh, aye." She straightens and aims those stunning blue eyes at me. "I have three brothers and two sisters."

"Five siblings? Blimey. Do you get on with all of them?"

"We get on very well. Lachlan and Rory, my oldest brothers, can be overprotective, but they mean well. I'm the fourth oldest, after my sister Fiona. Aidan and Jamie are the youngest."

"Fascinating." I tear my focus away from her eyes and force myself to study the menu again.

"Do you have brothers or sisters?"

Every ounce of blood in my body freezes. My fingers curl, the nails scraping the vinyl cover of the menu. I never react this way when someone asks me that question, but I think I...don't want to lie to Catriona. It's an unprecedented feeling. Since I can't tell her the truth, I resort to a little more deflection. "Do you have any other family? Parents? Aunts? Cousins?"

"Yes, I have many of those."

"Tell me about them. I'm fascinated by your family dynamic."

She says nothing for several seconds. When I glance at her, expecting to find the lass browsing the menu, instead I catch her staring intently at me. I recognize that look. It means the person I'm with wants to understand me, but no one can accomplish that feat.

"My cousin Logan is in the army," she says. "And my cousin Iain is an archaeologist. Watching him work inspired me to take a similar path."

"You're studying archaeology, correct?"

"Aye. I told you that in your office earlier."

"Did you? My brain is a bit muddled, apparently." Because she's so beautiful that I can't think.

Catriona laughs, the sound so delicate and sweet that I want to kiss her. "I asked you for advice."

"Oh. Well, I assumed you picked me at random because we met on that park bench."

"I chose you because—" She bites her lip. "Because you seemed so nice, and you were reading an archaeology textbook."

"Ah, I see." At least now I understand her reasons for insisting on getting to know me. Yes, I can be mates with Catriona Mac-Taggart. That won't result in a catastrophe.

Probably not.

I listen while Catriona tells me more about her siblings and cousins, and she grows more animated with every passing moment. Her smile is bright, her eyes sparkle, and her voice entrances me. Have I ever been as cheerful as she is? Of course I haven't. I am not the sort who gets a happily ever after ending. My story will conclude in a far darker manner. But the lovely lass beside me never needs to know who I really am or why I'm hiding in America, much less what I've done.

Neither of us order oysters, though we do both choose seafood entrées. Considering everything she shared with me, I feel uneasy about not telling her anything about myself. But I stay away from the issues of family and my background, instead relating humorous stories from my adventures as a PhD candidate and an associate professor. She loves the tale of the only time I participated in a field expedition and wound up falling into a river while trying to rescue what I thought was an artifact. It turned out to be a plastic hair clip.

"At least you didn't drown," Catriona says. "That would've been a right shame."

"Would it? I am an arse of the first order, so perhaps I deserved to drown."

Her smile disintegrates. "Why do you call yourself an arse of the first order?"

Oh, bollocks. I've committed the one error I never make. I let my guard down. "It was a joke, darling, that's all."

Her lips curl up at the corners, dimpling her cheeks. "I like that."

"What? That my jokes are bloody awful?"

"No. That you called me darling."

I can't come up with even one syllable in response. Maybe I call my anonymous lovers that, but I don't mean it in a romantic way. How did I mean it when I referred to Catriona that way? I have no fucking idea. "I'm glad you liked it, but I call every woman 'darling.' It's a British thing."

"Hmm." She eyes me with the most adorably fake expression of disapproval. "I donnae think I believe you, Alex. You're full of rubbish, aren't you?"

"Often and unrepentantly. You'd be better off finding someone else to take as your friend."

"No, I'm happy with you." She spears her fork into the last bite of her fish. "I like being with you. Haven't laughed this much in a long time."

"Neither have I." Maybe I've never enjoyed myself this much before. The thought is…unsettling. "I should take you home. It's getting late, and we both have classes in the morning."

I pay the bill, and we make our way out of the dining room into the entryway with its twilight ambiance. Catriona needs to use the ladies room, so I wait for her in a secluded space, leaning against the wall while I wonder what has happened to me. Dating a grad student? Dating, full stop? I never do that. Can't risk it. But since the moment I first saw Catriona, I've had no willpower to stay away from her.

She emerges from the loo and slips her hand into mine, smiling with what seems for all the world like affection.

I can't make myself shake her hand off. I push away from the wall, meaning to walk out the door, but then I stop and turn toward her. She is so bloody beautiful, and a need to taste her lips just once before I cut her out of my life grips me so hard that I can't breathe.

"What's wrong, Alex?" she asks.

The words she spoke barely penetrate my brain, and I can't stop myself. I back her up to the wall, cover her body with mine, and lift her hands to press them to the wall at either side of her shoulders. Her eyes flare wide, then drift half-closed. The sensual curve of her lips shatters my self-control. I crush my mouth to hers and plunge my tongue between her lips, diving deep to devour the flavor of her. Her breathy moan makes my cock jerk, and the feel of her breasts mounded against my chest makes me groan. I rock my hips to rub my growing erection into her belly even while I consume her mouth as if she is the only nourishment that can sustain me.

When I finally relinquish her lips, I can do nothing except stare at her.

She stares right back at me, but then her mouth curls into a sexy smile.

"Catriona, I—" What can I say? I'd meant to go out to my car and drop her off at her apartment, not molest the woman in the restaurant entryway. "I'm sorry."

"For what? I loved that kiss."

So did I. But I can't admit to that. "I need to take you home."

I lay a palm on her back to guide her out of the building and to my car. Neither of us speak on the ride to her flat, and though I walk her to her door, I do not kiss her good night. She seems confused when I don't even look her in the eye. I've just turned away, about to start back down the walkway, when she grasps my arm.

"Alex, wait."

Don't look at her. The only response I can safely give her is to revert to my old cavalier persona in a desperate attempt to escape. I do not glance at her even when I say, "If you were expecting me to fall madly in love with you after one mediocre kiss, I'm afraid you will be disappointed."

"If you want to chase me away, you'll at least have to look at me first."

Of course she insists I look at her. The Scots lass I'd taken for a shy girl has turned out to be the opposite. When I turn to face her, she gazes at me with nothing like shyness. A fire burns in her gaze, and I swear I can feel the heat penetrating my soul. That makes me want her even more.

"Happy now?" I say. "You wanted me to look at you before I tell you to bugger off, and I've done it. Dinner with you was a pleasant distraction, but I'm tired of you now."

I just stop myself from wincing when I speak those words. I'd meant it when I told my anonymous bedmate I was tired of her, but I'm lying to Catriona.

"*Mhac na galla*," she hisses. "You are the most obstinate man on earth. I donnae believe you, Alex, and I am going to figure out why you're so afraid to be with me."

"What was that phrase you spoke? It sounded like gibberish."

She bars her arms over her chest. "Never mind what it means. That was a curse, aimed at you because you're an eejit if you think I'll believe your insulting claim that kissing me was mediocre."

"Afraid it was, darling. Ta-ta."

I walk away, rather too swiftly, and trip over a seam in the concrete walkway. By the time I reach my car, my hands are shaking. It's ridiculous. By tomorrow, I will have forgotten about Catriona MacTaggart.

She will never haunt me again.

Chapter Four

Catriona

I attend class the next day, but I don't hear the lecture despite the fact the subject matter is of interest to me. Why can't I concentrate? Because of that *bod ceann*, Alex Thorne. Aye, he is a dickhead. Why else would he try to chase me away with insulting sarcasm? Something about kissing me terrified him. I've seen other men respond that way to intimacy, but I have never known anyone to say he's "tired" of me afterward. Is it any wonder why I cursed at him in Gaelic, calling the erse a son of a bitch?

That kiss had been bloody amazing.

Yet Alex wants me to believe it meant nothing to him. The way his left eyelid twitched when he said that convinced me that he didn't mean a word of it.

Why is Alex afraid to like me?

After class, I go to his office. But he isn't there. I check the schedule of classes on the university website and learn the *bod ceann* is teaching a class on British archaeology right now. So I head for Alex's classroom, though I don't go inside. I peer through the small window on the door which lets me see Alex where he stands at the front of the medium-size room. It's not as enormous as the lecture hall he'd used yesterday, but I assume British archaeology isn't as popular as his world history class. After all, that course is aimed at undergraduates, but the one today is for grad students.

While I watch secretly, Alex grows more animated as he lectures to his captive audience. He even grins when a student asks him a question. I wonder what the lass asked, because he clearly loves answering her question. The entire class laughs at something he said.

Alex Thorne might be a *bod ceann*, but he's also the most captivating teacher I've ever seen. Maybe I can't hear his lecture right now, but I sat in during his entire presentation yesterday. Alex is magnetic, electric, and completely mesmerizing.

But he pushed me away.

When did I become a coward? I have three large brothers, and I handle them quite well. I might have been nervous around Alex at first, but only because I have never been as attracted to any man as I am with Alex. Now that I've seen other sides of him, thanks to our intimate dinner last night, I no longer feel shy in his presence.

I watch Alex for a moment longer, then I hurry back to his office to wait for him. I sit down in the chair in front of his desk and watch the clock on the wall opposite me. His class should be ending in a few minutes. I resist the impulse to snoop in his office. I desperately want to do that because I need to understand why he behaves the way he does. But I'll need every ounce of patience I possess to solve the mystery of Alex Thorne.

Footsteps draw closer, and I glimpse the figure of Alex reflected in the window. He turns to the side as if he's thinking about sneaking away.

I crane my neck to glance back at him and smile. "Hello, Alex."

"Catriona." He speaks my name haltingly, as if he can't believe it's actually me. "Why are you here?"

"It's wonderful to see you too." I stand and face him. "I thought we should talk about last night."

"Whatever for? It was a pleasant distract—"

"No, Alex. I want to talk about *us*."

He scratches under his shirt collar. "There is no 'us.' There's me, there's you, and nothing between us."

"You kissed me."

"Do you stalk every bloke who kisses you?"

"Alex, please—"

He spreads an arm as if encouraging me to walk out the door. "I have a job to do. Goodbye, Catriona."

Alex won't talk to me. I have no choice but to leave.

Maybe I'm better off forgetting about Alex Thorne. Whatever his problems are, I need to focus on my studies and not the infernal man who kissed me, then called it mediocre and implied the experience was meaningless.

So that's what I do all week long. Occasionally, I pass by Alex's office and see him hunched over his desk studying papers. That posture doesn't seem like a sign of relaxation or happiness. He looks miserable. But I make some friends, and one lad even flirts with me. But I donnae feel anything for him other than platonic friendship. He seems fine with that, though the lad still flirts. Maybe "friends" isn't the right word to describe the other students I meet. They don't invite me to go anywhere with them, but we chat to each other in class. The lad who wants to date me sometimes approaches me on the quad when I'm reading or writing papers. Sooner or later, he will give up.

One day, I'm eating my lunch on the same bench where I'd met Alex when that boy, Aaron, sits down beside me.

"Hey, Catriona," he says. "You look really pretty today."

"Thank you." I don't even lift my head to look at him since I don't want to encourage the lad.

"What do I have to do to get you to go out with me?"

Morph into Alex Thorne, that's what. It's pathetic, but I can't stop thinking about that infuriating man. "I'm too busy to date, Aaron."

"Are you, like, a lesbian? I'm cool with that if you are. My half-sister is gay."

"No, I'm not a lesbian." I just don't want *him*.

I notice movement out of the corner of my eye, but it's not Aaron. The flash originated from the other direction. When I swivel my eyes toward the movement, I glimpse Alex spinning around to rush away.

What is he doing now?

I sling my rucksack over one shoulder and stand up. "It was nice to see you again, Aaron. Goodbye."

Though I would rather turn left, away from where I'd seen Alex, the classroom where I need to be in fifteen minutes is to my right. I won't see Alex. He ran away when he spotted me on the bench with Aaron. So I forget about him and walk down the concrete path. Halfway to my destination, I stop.

Because Alex is leaning against a tree, staring down at the ground with his hands jammed in his trouser pockets.

He looks so forlorn that I want to hug him. But he threw me over the other night, which means I owe him nothing. He'd been so sweet and charming during our dinner, and I'd loved that side of him. Do I want to get involved with a man who is clearly damaged by things he refuses to talk about? If I want a boyfriend, I can find someone less complicated.

Alex lifts his head and sees me. His head jerks back, and his eyes widen.

I have two choices—continue past him as if he doesn't exist, or stop and speak to him. Since I've never been good at shunning people, I approach the pitiful man. "Hello, Alex. How are you today?"

"Are you dating that child?" He doesn't sound angry. No, his voice is rife with pain.

"Do you mean Aaron? He's not a child. We're both working on our PhDs."

"You *are* dating him, then."

"No."

"But you've shagged him."

I shake my head. "Stop it, Alex. If you don't want to be with me, then you have no right to interrogate me about who I spend time with."

He bows his head and grips his nape. "I'm sorry. This is none of my concern."

Walk away, my logical brain tells me. But my heart urges me to find out what's fashing him. I inch closer. "Look at me, Alex, please."

He sighs, straightens, and clears his throat as he meets my gaze. "You're better off without me."

"Isn't that my decision?"

"You have no idea what you'd be letting yourself in for if you get involved with me."

"What have you done that's so awful?"

"It's complicated." He raises a hand as if to touch me but yanks it away. "I want you, Catriona. But I can't—You shouldn't want me."

"Alex—"

He takes off across the grass, making a beeline for the humanities building at the opposite end of the quad from where I need to go. Why do I care if Alex feels bad? He treated me wonderfully at first, then turned around and tossed me away like so much rubbish. I wish I hadn't seen the pain in his eyes when he'd done that or heard the tension in his voice when he told me our kiss had meant nothing. But I did see and hear that. And I can't help that I want to know more about him, to find out what has made him so afraid to get close to me.

I should forget about him. I *will* forget about him.

That evening, I'm sitting in my living room watching a bad television show when the doorbell rings. I yawn and stretch, then pad over to the door. Who would want to see me at nine o'clock? I don't really know anyone in this country, not anyone who would stop by at such a late hour. But I peek through the peephole—and freeze.

It's Alex.

Maybe I shouldn't do it, but I cannae stop myself from opening the door. "What are you doing here?"

Alex leans against the jamb, giving me that sexy half smile I'd seen often during our one and only date. "I wanted to apologize. In person. May I come in?"

I chew on my lip for a moment while I consider how to respond. He looks delicious in casual clothes—jeans and a polo shirt—but I cannae let my hormones make this decision. My heart does that instead. "Aye, you can come in."

Stepping aside, I wait until he's crossed the threshold, then shut the door. I'm completely alone with him. A man I barely know. Yet I trust him. Why? Not a bloody clue. He hesitates halfway to the sofa, seeming unsure of what to do now.

"Go on, sit down," I say as I wave toward the sofa and the armchair. "Wherever you like."

He drops onto the nearest end of the sofa.

I sit at the other end. "Did you have a reason for coming here?"

"Yes, of course." He sets his hands on his knees and curls his fingers over them. "I've behaved horribly. You have every right to tell me to sod off, but I hope you won't."

"Why would I tell you to do that?"

He glances at me sideways, almost smirking but not quite. "You wouldn't, naturally. I'm the arse would say something like that. I did say something similar to you after our date. I want to apologize for that, Catriona. I loved spending time with you—and kissing you."

"So it wasn't mediocre after all."

"No." He turns his face toward me. "It was the most incredible kiss I've ever experienced. I'm sorry for everything I said after I drove you home."

"Apology accepted."

His brows cinch up, and his lips fall open. "Why are you forgiving me?"

"Because I believe you're sincere, and everyone deserves a second chance."

"Everyone? Not sure that's true."

I'm about to ask why he thinks that, but then he yawns and sags into the sofa, letting his head fall back against it as he shuts his eyes. He looks so exhausted that I donnae have the heart to question him anymore tonight.

"You seem too jeeked to drive home," I say.

He peels one eye open to look at me. "Jeeked?"

"It means you're exhausted."

"Oh. Yes, I am that." He blows out a sigh and closes both eyes again. "This sofa is so comfortable that I think I could sleep for a thousand years."

"Why don't you sleep on the sofa tonight?" Did I just invite him to spend the night? Aye, and I meant it. Maybe being away from my entire family and living in another country has driven me off my head, because I don't regret making that offer.

Alex rotates his head toward me, and his caramel eyes zero in on me. "Are you sure you want me to do that? Stay the night, I mean."

"Yes, Alex, I'm sure. Cannae have you careening off the road on your way home."

He stares at me. "Thank you, Catriona."

"You can call me Cat if you like. It's my nickname."

"Thank you, Cat."

His eyes drift shut again, though his head stays turned to the side. I crawl on my knees until I'm right beside him, then raise my hand as if to caress his face, but I stop. Maybe I shouldn't touch him. Maybe I ought to ring for a taxi to take him home. But he looks so innocent and sweet right now, not at all like the way he'd behaved after our date. So I give in and spread my palm over his cheek, sliding it across his skin and into his hair.

One of his eyes opens partway. "What are you doing?"

"Hush." I begin combing my fingers through his hair in a gentle rhythm. "I'm trying to help you relax."

"Mm." His lid falls shut. "It's working."

He sounds very sleepy, but I keep brushing his hair with my fingertips until his breathing grows shallow and regular. I think he's asleep, or at least almost there. I carefully slide off the sofa and tiptoe into my bedroom to retrieve a blanket, then I return to the sofa.

Alex now lies stretched along the sofa's length, his shoes on the floor and his eyes closed.

I drape the blanket over him and grab a throw pillow which I gently tuck under his head. He doesn't even stir. I gaze down at him for a moment, then I lean in to kiss his cheek. He seems almost angelic in sleep, as if all his worries have evaporated.

Back in my bedroom, I change into a nightie and crawl under the covers. But I can't stop thinking about one question.

What will I do with Alex Thorne?

Chapter Five

Alex

I wake in the morning feeling rather good. Much better than yesterday, for sure. Catriona has forgiven me for my abominable behavior, and for some reason, that makes me feel bloody fantastic. She tucked me in last night too. I doubt she realized I was only half-asleep, but I'd been just awake enough to feel it when she kissed my cheek.

Only one other woman has ever done that, and she wasn't even my lover. Catriona isn't either, though I want her to be that and so much more. I don't deserve this kind of chance with this kind of woman, but I will take whatever she offers me.

The past be damned.

I suddenly realize today is Saturday, which means I have the entire weekend with Catriona, if she wants me to stay for that long.

Since her bedroom door is closed, I decide she must be sleeping. In the kitchen, I find all the ingredients I need to cook a decent breakfast for her. I'm hardly a gourmet chef, but I know how to make edible food. I've just gathered everything I need when Catriona sashays out of her bedroom wearing nothing but a blue nightie. Its spaghetti straps and short hemline give me a tantalizing view of her thighs and the slopes of her breasts.

"Good morning, darling," I say, with no sarcasm at all when I speak that word. "Are you hungry?"

Catriona halts mid-step. She lifts her head to gawp at me. "Alex? Why are you—" She winces. "I invited you to stay."

"And you clearly forgot about that when you woke up this morning." I rove my gaze over her from head to toe and back again. "You should dress this way more often."

"It's a nightie, Alex. I only dress this way at night."

"That's a shame, love. You are even more stunning barely clothed and mussed from sleep."

"Mussed?" She pats her hair and winces again. "I forgot to brush my hair."

"I know, and I like it. Nothing is sexier than a tousled woman in a skimpy negligee." I can't resist smirking. "Well, except for a nude woman."

"Donnae get ahead of yourself, Alex."

"Why not? It's my default position."

Catriona ambles up to the kitchen bar and perches on a stool. "What are you cooking?"

"I was planning to make you a decadent feast." I survey the ingredients I'd laid out. "But now I'm getting a different idea."

"You don't need to make a fuss. Honestly, scrambled eggs are fine with me."

"That's not what I meant." My focus gravitates to her chest and the tantalizing slopes of those generous breasts. "It's your choice, darling. Would you rather eat breakfast or make love?"

She stares blankly at me.

Well, I did warn her that going too far is my default position. I've wanted her since the moment we met, and now we're alone in her flat. We've already kissed once, and she invited me to spend the night on her sofa. So I'm hoping she wants what I want.

I raise my brows at her. "Is the decision that difficult?"

"No." She hops off her stool and sashays around to my side of the counter, stopping an arm's length away. "Let's make love, Alex."

For two seconds, I assume I've misheard her. Then she drags her tongue across her lips and moves her fingers over her chest in slow circles. Oh no, I did not misunderstand her.

I grasp her hips and tug her closer. "I'm glad you said that, because I need to fuck you right now."

"What happened to making love?"

"Don't worry, we'll do that too. I mean to give us both a workout before breakfast."

"I'd love that." She cocks her head as if she wants to study me. "Were you lying when you said calling me 'darling' meant nothing?"

"Yes, I was. I am a bloody liar, sometimes. So before we do this, you should understand a few things about me."

Catriona slips her arms around my waist and snuggles up to me. "I'm listening."

"In all my life, I have never made love to a woman. I only shag them."

"Am I meant to be shocked? I can handle that, Alex."

Maybe she can, and I hope I won't need to test that faith. "I will never tell you about my past or my family."

"Why not?"

"Because I won't. If that's a deal breaker for you, then I will walk out the door and never bother you again."

She chews on her upper lip while scrutinizing me again. Just when I think she'll tell me to bugger off, she kisses me instead. Sweetly. On the lips only. Then she smiles. "I agree to your terms."

"They're not terms. They're facts of life with me."

"And I agree to your facts."

Why on earth she wants to live with my limitations, I cannot fathom. But she knows what I can't give her, and she still said yes.

Catriona wriggles against me. "I've never slept with a man I met less than a week ago."

"You still haven't. I slept on the sofa, and you slept in the bedroom." I lay my palms on her arse. "And if I have my way, we won't be sleeping this morning, either."

"You know what I meant."

Oh yes, I know. "Last chance to change your mind."

"Are we going to have a poke today? Or will ye keep trying to change my mind until next Wednesday?"

I sweep her up in my arms. "Does this answer your question?"

She laughs.

God, she's beautiful. And so sweet that I want to hold her in my arms forever. But my cock disapproves of that idea, so I carry her into the bedroom and set her down at the foot of the bed. "Shall I undress you? Or would you rather strip for me?"

Catriona bites her lip in that shy yet sexy way I've seen before. Does she realize how desirable she is? I doubt that. She's probably dated men her own age, which means twats who have no idea what to do with a real woman.

"How old are you?" I ask.

"Twenty-four. How old are you?"

"I'm twenty-nine."

She leans into me. "Were you worried I'm not legal?"

"No, darling. You're a grad student, so I was reasonably sure I wouldn't get arrested for shagging you. I was curious, that's all."

The lovely lass takes hold of the hem of her flimsy nightie. "I'll undress myself."

I take a few steps backward. "Go on, Cat. Strip for me. Though it won't take long considering how little you're wearing."

She pulls the nightie over her head and tosses it away, which leaves her standing completely nude. I couldn't look away from her if I tried, not that I want to do that. Her full breasts capture all of my attention, and I can't help fantasizing about touching and tasting them. Fuck, she's perfect. Her creamy skin is sprinkled with the faintest freckles, including one on her left nipple. She has the best combination of muscle tone and womanly softness, from her slender waist to her wide hips and down to her thighs that seem strong enough to grip me while I fuck her.

"Cat, you are exquisite."

She smiles shyly.

And that makes me want her even more. But it's my turn now, and I get rid of my clothes as fast as possible because I feel like I might explode if I don't start touching her right now. I yank the covers off the bed. "Lie down, love. On your back."

She obeys, and I crawl up the bed on my hands and knees until my face hovers directly over hers. She reaches up to touch her fingertips to my mouth. I kiss her fingers one by one, then lunge my head down to claim her lips, kissing her with a sort of abandon I've never experienced before. I don't generally kiss the women I shag, but with Cat, I need to taste her mouth and explore every silky corner of it before I devour the rest of her.

I pull my mouth away, now breathing harder. "When was the last time a man went down on you?"

She hunches her shoulders. "Never."

"Never? What sort of arses do you date?"

"Boys don't like to do that."

"Are these American arses or Scottish ones?"

She lays a hand on my cheek while smiling at me like I'm the daftest man on earth. "Scottish ones. I only moved to America two weeks ago. You're the first not-Scottish man I've been with."

"I see. Scotsmen don't know how to pleasure women. Can't say that surprises me. After all, they do wear plaid obsessively, and they love those horrid bagpipes."

"Oh, one day you will regret saying that. My three large brothers love to wear kilts—and toss cabers."

"Could we not discuss your brothers while we're naked in bed?"

"Aye." She makes a zipper motion across her lips.

"Feel free to speak. Just not about your brothers. I will be very disappointed if you don't at least scream my name."

She giggles. If any other woman did that, I would've thought it was moronic. But when Cat giggles, it's the most charming thing in the world. "I donnae even scream on roller coasters, Alex."

"Oh, but I'm going to give you pleasure beyond your wildest dreams." When she starts to speak, I seal her lips with one finger. "Wait and see."

I crawl backward until my head is aligned with her hips, then I lower myself onto my belly. My face lies just over the soft, curly hairs of her mound. "Spread your legs and bend your knees, pet."

She does that without any hesitation. Cat trusts me. She must, otherwise she wouldn't have let me stay the night, much less let me make love to her. Do I trust her? I suppose I must. Never have I let anyone get as close to me as Catriona has done. Well, no one except for the only two people in the world who really know me.

I nuzzle her mound. "You smell so fucking good, Cat. I can't wait to taste you."

She's breathing harder, her breasts rising and falling.

With two fingers, I separate her folds to expose the rigid nub of her clitoris, surrounded by the glistening evidence of her lust for me. "I'm going to lick up every last drop of your cream."

I push my face between her thighs and devour her with quick swipes of my tongue, though I avoid her clit for now. Instead, I lick my way down one side of her folds and flick my tongue into her opening before I lick my way up the other side. Cat gasps and writhes beneath me, fisting her hands in the pillow while her neck arches. My breathing has accelerated too, along with my pulse. My cock had been marginally firm when we lay down on the bed, but now it feels like it might explode if I don't shag her in the next thirty seconds.

I never rush, though—especially not with Cat.

"Alex," she moans as I latch on to her clit and suckle it. "Oh God, yes."

The flavor of her suffuses my mouth and makes me feel almost drunk. I need to push her over the edge now, before I come all over her flower-print sheets. So I plunge two fingers inside her and pump while ravishing her nub.

Her body goes rigid an instant before the first spasms grip my fingers. She cries out just as her body bows inward, and she squeezes her eyes shut while I keep finger-fucking her until she collapses onto the mattress. "Alex…"

I rise to my knees. "We aren't done yet."

She gives me a smile so charming and sexy that my cock throbs. "You are as good as you think."

"Am I? Perhaps you should wait until I'm done before making a pronouncement like that." I glance around to look for my trousers, but then I realize we have a problem. My head falls forward as I groan. "I don't have a condom."

"Donnae worry. I have one." She twists her upper body to reach the nightstand and pull the drawer open. Then she tosses me a condom packet. "See? No problem."

"Why do you have condoms? I thought you hadn't been with anyone since you moved here."

"I haven't. But I believe in being prepared. I have packets in my purse too."

"You are wonderful, Cat."

She laughs.

And I get the condom on as quickly as I can. Then I plant my hands on the mattress at either side of her shoulders and thrust inside her lush body. She feels even better than I'd imagined, despite the condom. Her heat surrounds me, and her hairs tickle my skin as I begin a measured pace. We gaze into each other's eyes the entire time, and the glacial blue of her irises seems darker and more intense thanks to the dilation of her pupils. Understanding the physiology of that does nothing to diminish the beauty of her eyes. Faint pinkness dapples her cheeks as her lips fall open and her breaths quicken.

I'm breathing harder and faster too. Though I'd love to stay nestled inside her forever, the pressure inside me grows with every thrust, and I know I won't last much longer. So I reach down to rub her clit, pistoning my hips faster, plunging deeper with every inward lunge.

Cat gasps and grips the headboard rails. "Yes, Alex, yes. Donnae stop."

With a strangled cry, she comes.

Even as her body milks me with pulsating spasms, I keep punching into her, knowing I'll explode any second. The bed creaks and thumps as I thrust wildly with both palms flat on the mattress. Everything inside me feels like I'm on a roller coaster that's crawling up the highest hill and I'm about to crest it. I can't stop myself from pounding into Cat while the tension escalates so much that the breath freezes in my lungs.

Then I hit that peak and roar down the slope in free-fall.

I come so hard I can't even shout. But my body takes over since my brain has shut down, and it forces me to pump into her a few more times as sweat dribbles down my temples. When I finally collapse onto the bed next to Cat, making the mattress bounce, I'm fighting to catch my breath.

The lovely lass beside me is struggling to breathe too.

Once I've recovered my wits, I roll onto my side to drape an arm over her belly. "That was incredible, Cat."

"Aye, it was." She rolls over too, her delectable body rubbing against mine. "How soon can we do that again?"

I chuckle.

Chapter Six

Catriona

Why are you laughing?" I ask. When Alex only smirks at me, I flip onto my back and fold my arms over my breasts. "You said it was incredible, but now you're acting like you think sex with me is hilarious. I donnae understand men at all."

"No, you clearly don't." He slings an arm over my belly and kisses me. "I gather the blokes you shagged didn't stay for round two. Did they at least spend the night with you?"

I shrug. "They usually said they had to get up early for work and didn't want to bother with setting an alarm for an earlier time just so they could go home and change clothes."

"Bother? Sleeping with a woman is not a nuisance. Waking up with one isn't either."

"You said you only shag women. You don't sleep with them."

"Well, yes…" He bows his head and scratches the back of it. Then he peeks up at me through his thick lashes. "But now I want to do that—with you. And I want to make love to you over and over too."

"Then why did ye laugh when I asked if we could do it again?"

"Men aren't machines, love. We need time to recover before we can have another go."

"How long does that take?"

Alex seals his open mouth over my belly button and blows out a breath. His lips vibrate my skin, and I start to giggle. Honestly, I never do that. But Alex knows exactly how to make me do silly things and love every minute of it. He also knows how to give me intense pleasure.

Alex kisses a path up my belly and straight to my throat, where he feathers his lips over my skin. "Why don't we have a light breakfast first? I'm sure I'll be up for it after that."

"I could eat a whole haggis by myself."

He feigns disgust. "I hope you don't expect me to kiss you after that. And I said light breakfast. We don't want to gorge ourselves right before sex."

"Men are finicky about this, aren't you?"

"It's biology, darling. I can't change that."

"All right. Breakfast first." I try to sit up, but he gently pushes me back down. "Stay here. I will bring you breakfast in bed."

"What should I do while I wait for you?"

"Anything you like." He pecks a kiss on my lips. "It will be worth the wait, I promise."

I watch Alex climb off the bed. Then he walks out the door, giving me a perfect view of his arse until he moves out of my sight. That man has a beautiful body and the face of an angel. But when he makes love to me, his expression turns into fierce hunger. I've never seen a man look like that during sex. I love it, and I cannae wait until we have another poke.

What should I do now? Alex suggested I should lie about in bed, but that's dead boring. I count the balls on the ceiling until I start to go cross-eyed, then I play thumb war with my own hands, which isn't very satisfying. The scent of food wafts into the bedroom, making my tummy rumble. Aye, I'm fair starved. Sex with Alex turned into an aerobic workout.

A sensuous warmth rushes through me as I flash back to a little while ago when Alex had been inside me. Poised over me. Thrusting and gasping, his expression the picture of intense need. He's always gorgeous, but in the throes, he becomes a god. I'm growing slick between my thighs again just from remembering what we did. My favorite bit was when he said in that rough, rumbly voice, "I'm going to lick up every last drop of your cream."

Now a tingling erupts between my thighs too.

I need him to fuck me again right now, but Alex insisted he cannae do that yet. Though I try not to, I cannae help fantasizing about those moments in this bed. The more I think about that, and him, the more I need to come. My clit throbs as I wriggle uncomfortably, afflicted with a growing need to relieve the pressure.

How long will it take Alex to make breakfast? I glance at the clock on the nightstand and realize it's only been ten minutes since he left the room. Cannae wait that long.

So I close my eyes and slip a finger between my folds to stroke myself while I imagine Alex licking me the way had earlier. Oh, his tongue. It had felt like velvet on my flesh. I move my finger in a rhythm that matches how he had devoured me, and excitement rises inside me. My back arches. I moan his name and rub faster.

"Bloody hell, Cat. Don't get started without me."

My eyes fly open. I stare at Alex, feeling strangely embarrassed that he caught me. After what we did earlier, I donnae know how I can feel that way, but I do. "Alex. What are you doing?"

He's not holding a tray of food. He just stands in the doorway gawping at me.

Alex clears his throat. "I, ah, wanted to know if you prefer your eggs fried or scrambled."

"Oh. Scrambled." Just like my brain.

"Good. I'll, ah, go finish cooking everything." He turns away, then glances over his shoulder at me. And he smirks. "No cheating, love. You are not to come until I say so."

Normally, I don't like bossy men. But when Alex commands me not to come, I obey because I love everything he does to me. Still, I'm a wee bit fashed that I need to wait for my next orgasm. At least with Alex, I know it will be worth the wait.

I'm having sex with a man I barely know. My family would be horrified if they found out, but I donnae need to tell them everything. I'm a grown woman who can make her own decisions. And I've decided to be with Alex Thorne.

He returns a few minutes later carrying a tray of food. "Sit up, darling. You can't eat lying down."

I push up into a sitting position and grab the top sheet to pull it over me.

Alex sets the tray on my lap. "Go ahead and start eating. I'll join you momentarily."

Before I have the chance to ask where he's going, he strides around to the other side of the bed and climbs in beside me.

"I thought you meant you were leaving the room," I say. "But you're still here."

"Did you want me to leave?"

"No. I like having you here."

He picks up a cherry tomato and slips it between my lips. "I assumed we would share the food."

I eat the tomato and kiss him. "I'd love to do that."

We enjoy our shared meal, feeding each other bits of food and making jokes so often that it takes us an hour to finish. It's hard to chew while laughing. I've never had this much fun with a man before. Well, my brothers are entertaining too, and so are my male cousins. But the fun Alex and I have together is different. None of the other men I dated wanted to enjoy this kind of intimacy with me. Sharing a meal while naked? No, they wanted to leave as soon as we had a poke. They didn't even stay a few minutes to cuddle.

But Alex, the man who confounded me all week long with his strange behavior, seems to be in no hurry to leave this bed.

After setting the tray on the floor, Alex whips the sheet off to expose our naked bodies—and his growing erection. "Shall we have another poke, my bonnie Scots lass?"

I laugh. "Aye, we should."

He called me his lass. I like that.

We spend the rest of the morning in bed, though not asleep. Alex knows how to turn sex into a workout, but then he'll turn around and make love to me with such tenderness that I get a strange pang in my chest. It's not a bad feeling.

In the afternoon, we go sightseeing since neither of us know the city well. Ballesteros lies in the mountains rather than the desert, so it has grass and conifer forests. When I decided to do my PhD program here, I'd expected that all of New Mexico must be flat and dry, but I was wrong. I'd looked up pictures of the area on the internet while planning my move, and the landscape had intrigued me.

When I tell Alex that, as we're driving down the road, he chuckles. "You moved to another country for the trees. Cat, you are adorable."

"Not only for the trees. I liked the mountains too."

"Well, that makes sense, of course."

He's teasing me, but I love that. Since Alex is driving, I decide to tease him in return.

I lay a hand on his thigh and slide it up toward his groin. "Why did you move to New Mexico?"

"Not for the ruddy trees, that's for sure." He grimaces when I move my hand a wee bit higher, grazing his cock. "But I'd be happy to fuck you in the woods if that's what turns you on."

"What turns me on is you."

He glances at me and smirks, though I can't see his eyes because he's wearing sunglasses. "Better remove your charming little hand from my leg, darling. If I develop an erection, I won't bother pulling over to the side of the road to shag you. I'll do it while the car is moving, and I can't swear we won't cause a mile-long pileup."

I pull my hand away and laugh. "Eyes on the road, Alex."

"You are so provincial."

We stay in town for our first joint sightseeing trip, but Ballesteros has plenty of fun ways to spend an afternoon. We visit a wee museum dedicated to the town's history. I love history, of course, since I'm a student of archaeology. But I have trouble focusing on the displays. My attention keeps drifting back to Alex. He's so animated while he talks about the artifacts in glass cases, waving his hands and making the cutest expressions. I have trouble reconciling this Alex with the man who had told me our first kiss was "mediocre" and who had seemed so melancholy when he saw me speaking to another man.

Aye, he's complicated. One day I will ask him to explain his behavior, but I don't want to do that just yet. I'm loving this version of him, and asking questions might send him into another downward spiral.

I shouldn't care for him, not yet, but I do.

We spend the entire weekend together, both of us sleeping in my bed at night. On Monday morning, I wake up before Alex does and just lie here watching him sleep. Does he dream about me? I dream about him, but not in the way I'd expected. Instead of having steamy dreams about him, my nighttime fantasies involve Alex enfolding me in his arms, smiling at me, holding my hand as we take a walk together. Those dreams might be more dangerous than the erotic sort.

Alex rouses and yawns, stretching his arms above his head. "Good morning, love. Did you sleep well?"

"Very well, thank you."

He lifts an arm as an invitation to cuddle up to him, and I happily accept that offer. "I'm afraid it's back to the grindstone today. But maybe we could have lunch together."

"I have a free hour at noon."

"So do I." He kisses the top of my head. "Meet me on our bench at twelve o'clock. I'll bring the food."

We lounge in bed for a few more minutes, but then it's time to start the day. After having a shower with Alex, one that does not involve sex, I make breakfast while he teases me about feeding him pancakes instead of something Scottish. When I suggest I could make him haggis for lunch, he pretends to gag, then grins at me in the way that always makes my pulse beat faster.

We take Alex's car, which means we can park in the faculty lot instead of in the boondocks where students are allowed to park. Before he gets out of the car, we kiss. It's not a sweet kiss either, but a steamy one that leaves me feeling wonderfully warm and tingly.

Hand in hand, we amble down the concrete paths until we reach the intersection where he needs to turn left and I need to turn right. Even after we go our separate ways, we keep glancing back at each other and grinning. What is this tingly sensation I'm feeling? Why does his smile make warmth blossom in my chest? The answer is dead obvious, and it doesn't frighten me the way I'd expected it should.

Oh, aye. I'm falling for Alex Thorne.

Chapter Seven

Alex

Catriona MacTaggart has cast a spell over me. I have no other explanation for what I've done or what I plan to do moving forward. I mean to go on behaving in a ridiculous manner, which means tickling her belly until she's laughing so hard that tears roll down her cheeks, teasing her about haggis, and making love to her as often as possible for as long as possible.

I didn't only spend the night with her. I stayed for the entire weekend. Even worse, I did nothing except play silly buggers with her. Can't remember the last time I took time off simply to…have fun. I work, I shag anonymous women, I eat, I sleep, and I go back to work. Christ, what a dull existence I've carved out for myself.

Not anymore. A single weekend with Cat has given me something I never thought I wanted—happiness.

It will all go pear-shaped, eventually. It must. Someone like me does not deserve this kind of joy. Is that what I'm experiencing? Joy? I can honestly say it has never happened to me before. Maybe that explains why I suddenly find myself almost dancing down the path to the humanities building this morning, and worse, realize I'm whistling a cheerful tune. *Bloody hell.* I've become the sort of bloke I used to scoff at, one of those poor sods who loses his head over a pretty girl.

As I enter the building, I wonder what Cat is doing right now. She's taking a statistics course, which means she must be inside the mathematics building right now, listening to a boring lecture about percentages and calculations or whatever. I probably won't see her again until noon, when we have our lunch date.

"Good morning, Dr. Thorne."

I stop and turn around to face the man who spoke. The dean of my department gives me a pleasant smile, and I can't help smiling at him with genuine happiness for the first time in…ever. Well, I grinned at Cat all weekend, so it's not the actual first time.

"Good morning, Dean Wells," I say. "It's a lovely morning, isn't it?"

"Yes, it is." He studies me for a moment. "Don't think I've ever seen anybody look so happy on a Monday morning. What's your secret?"

Catriona is my secret elixir of happiness. But I tell the dean, "I had a wonderful weekend, that's all. I feel refreshed."

"Good for you." He pats my shoulder as he walks past me. "Whatever her name is, you're one lucky guy."

As the dean wanders off down the corridor, I stand immobilized. I am a lucky man. My life has changed in the space of a week, and I never want to go back to the way things were.

Though I teach my classes and grade papers the way I'm meant to do, my thoughts keep rewinding to the weekend and Cat and all the things we did together. Noon finally arrives, and I sit on the bench I've come to think of as ours, waiting for Catriona to stroll up the path. When I finally see her, I swear my heart skips a beat.

She smiles and waves at me.

And I get an odd twinge in my chest.

"What did you bring for lunch?" Cat asks as she sits down beside me. "I'm fair starved."

"Must be the aftereffects of two days of sex and sightseeing."

"I think so." She bumps her shoulder into mine. "I loved our weekend together."

"So did I." Reaching under the bench, I pull out the picnic basket I'd hidden under there. "Sorry. I didn't have time to cook for you, so I ordered a picnic for us from a restaurant."

Catriona rubs her palms together and licks her lips.

I chuckle. "You are adorably ravenous."

We enjoy our picnic while talking about nothing of consequence, unless secretly joking about what other people are wearing counts as an important discussion. On our way to the humanities building, I guide her off the path and into a secluded spot surrounded by bushes and trees, where no one will see us.

And then I kiss her.

She wraps her arms around my neck and moans. I need to kiss her all the time, to taste her and feel her body pressed to mine every moment of every day. But I can't do that. I'll have to resign myself to taking whatever I can get and making love to her every night.

For the next three weeks, we ignore the rest of the world as much as possible and just enjoy being together. The longer I'm with Cat, the more I want to keep her with me forever. Do I have the right to do that? Should I do it? She has no idea about my past, and I never want to explain that to her.

This weekend, I've invited Cat to stay in my loft. For me, that's a huge step and a huge risk, though it doesn't terrify me as much as what I mean to do next.

I drive Catriona to the outskirts of town where my apartment complex lies on a quiet street, surrounded by trees and set back off the road just enough that I can't see the street or the neighboring buildings. Yes, I cherish privacy. Cat's eyes widen as we walk through the entryway of my second-floor loft and continue into the living room.

"Are you rich, Alex?" she asks. "I've never seen a loft like this before."

She's referring to the posh furniture and the expensive lithographic prints on the walls, not to mention the Persian rugs on the floor. If she thinks I must be wealthy based on the living room decor, she will probably pass out when she sees the kitchen. Maybe one man doesn't need all these things. I can't explain why I felt an impulse to turn my apartment into something out of a model home show. I suppose it makes me feel safe.

"Well, Alex," she says, "are you rich?"

"Perhaps I have more money than some people. Does that matter to you?"

"No. But I'm curious about how you got so much money. Archaeology professors aren't usually millionaires."

"You could call it family money."

"I *could* call it that?" She turns to face me, raising her brows. "What does that mean?"

Rubbing my jaw, I try to think of a way to explain this without actually explaining it. "Family money means…family money. I inherited most of it and invested the rest to grow my assets."

"You inherited money from your parents?"

"Does it matter? I told you I won't discuss my past. It wouldn't be illuminating for you, anyway." I can tell she wants to interrogate me more, so I distract her by clasping her hand and guiding her into the kitchen. "I think you'll enjoy cooking in here, especially since you can see into the living room."

The open kitchen features a bar that sits just behind the living room, as well as every sort of kitchen gadget anyone could want but no one really needs. Cat ambles over to the large stand mixer on the counter and runs her fingers over the rim of its bowl. Then she glances at me sideways while smiling slightly in the manner I've realized means she thinks I'm being an "eejit." Yes, I am an idiot in many ways, particularly when it comes to stocking my kitchen with useless contraptions.

"Do you invite the entire faculty of Ballesteros University to dinner parties here?" she asks.

"No. I've never invited anyone to my home. I don't even let the FedEx man come inside."

"Then why do you need all these things?" She spreads an arm to indicate my outrageous collection of gadgets. "Ye donnae seem like the sort who loves technology."

"I have a mobile phone and a wide-screen TV."

She laughs in the soft and affectionate way I've heard often lately, the way I adore. "You are so cute when you're full of rubbish, Alex."

I pull her into me. "I also own an electric shiatsu massager. Care to try out that device?"

"Only if you're using it on me while we're naked."

"Naturally." I take her hand, leading her through the living and down a hallway to an open door. "This is my bedroom."

"May I go in there?"

"Have at it, love."

She races into the room and belly flops onto the bed, then flips over to move her arms and legs as if she's creating a snow angel on the comforter without any snow. My God, she is enchanting. I love every ridiculous thing she does, and watching her writhe around on the bed while grinning makes me want to tear her clothes off and fuck her.

But I have something to discuss with her first.

I sit down on the bed near her. "Could we talk for a moment?"

Catriona springs up into a sitting position and wriggles her lovely arse to get closer to me. "What did you want to talk about?"

"Well, ah..." I suddenly can't speak the words. That's bollocks. I always know what to say to a woman, how to maneuver anyone into my bed, but this is different. I don't want to seduce Cat. All right, I mean to do that too. But first, I need to tell her something I've never told anyone. I scratch my arms and feel my face pinching up. "Catriona, I—Uh, it's—"

She grasps my face and urges me to look at her. "Whatever it is, Alex, you can tell me. I won't run away."

Maybe she should run. But I can't bear the thought of losing her. So I suck in a breath and do it. "I'd like you to move in with me."

"Oh." She stares at me for a moment, then breaks into a grin. "Yes, Alex, I'd love to live with you."

Why? That's what I want to ask, but I won't cock this up by acting like an arse. I need her with me all the time, and she just agreed to share my home—and my bed. "There are a few things you need to know first. I've told you I won't talk about my past or my family."

"Aye, and I said that's all right."

"From this moment forward, I don't want to even think about the past. All that matters is us, our present and our future together."

"I agree."

Part of me still can't accept that she understands my rules and agrees to abide by them. If one day she grows tired of my limitations and leaves me… I won't think about that today. Or tomorrow. Or next month. I will relish having her with me for as long as I can.

"Are you hungry yet?" I ask. "Or should we delay dinner and shag instead?"

Her sexy smile melts my heart. "Sex first. And get the shiatsu massager."

"Anything for you, love."

For the next hour, I use that massager, as well as my mouth and hands, to drive Cat to multiple orgasms. Then she uses the device on me, but I can't resist flipping her over so I can shag her the right way—with my cock buried inside her.

After our exercise routine, we make dinner together.

Yes, I'm calling sex an exercise routine. It was very athletic, after all.

In the morning, we go to Cat's flat to retrieve her belongings. Then I take her to lunch at a nice restaurant. She plans to give up her flat so another student can have it since she doesn't need her own place anymore. We're living together. We are a couple. I expect to experience a twinge of panic whenever I think about what I've done, but I feel only good things.

Cat and I develop a routine of going to the grocery store on Saturday mornings and then having lunch at our favorite café. On this day, having just left the restaurant, we stroll down the sidewalk hand in hand, in no hurry to reach our car. Well, technically it›s my car since my name is on the registration. But I›ve come to think of it as ours. Catriona had hired a car when she first moved to Ball-esteros, and though she›d intended to buy one eventually, she never got round to it.

She stops me half a block from where we parked our car. "I need to use the restroom. In that shop behind us."

"You don't need my permission."

"Would you rather I ran off without explaining?"

"I see your point." Kissing her cheek, I release her hand. "Go on. I'll wait here."

The woman I adore hurries into the shop, and I shove my hands in my trouser pockets while I wait for her to return.

"I don't believe it," a feminine voice declares from behind me. "It's actually you."

That voice…I recognize it. Turning toward the woman, I can't help grimacing. If fate exists, it clearly despises me. Because the woman I shagged the night before I met Cat, the "I love your dick" idiot, is standing there grinning at me.

She sashays closer and speaks in a sultrier tone. "Imagine my luck bumping into you again. I'm staying in the big hotel near the freeway on-ramp."

Am I meant to give a toss where she's staying? I never knew her name and never wanted to see her again. Cat will come out of the shop at any moment, which means I need to shake this woman off quickly. "Sorry, I think you have me confused with someone else."

She wags a finger at me. "No, no, baby. I could never forget that face and those lips."

"Please bugger off," I say as if the woman means nothing to me, which is true. "I have no desire to speak to you and certainly no inclination to go anywhere with you."

The bloody woman pouts, though it's sheer artifice. "Come on, baby. We had so much fun together."

"I enjoyed the orgasms, not you." Yes, I feel like a wanker for say-ing that, though it wouldn't have bothered me before I met Cat. I have no choice right now. The tart won't leave unless I berate her. Then again, she might like that. "I said go away, darling. You can bat your eyelashes for the next hour, but it won't make me want you."

The bloody woman huffs and throws her hands up. "Fine. It's your loss."

At last, she ambles off down the sidewalk.

I rub my eyes with the heels of my hands and exhale a long sigh.

"Alex, who was that?"

When I remove my hands from my face, I can do nothing except stare at Cat. She's just walked out of the shop and seems rightfully baffled. I consider lying to her, but I don't want to do that. Instead, I approach her and clasp her hands. "That was a woman I shagged the night before I met you. It was just sex, and I spent only a couple of hours with her. It meant nothing."

"I understand. You have a past, and I can handle it." Her lips curl into a sweet little smile that dimples her cheeks. "Even if a horde of your former bedmates swarm me, I'll be fine."

"Why? I can't imagine any other woman would accept the way I used to be."

"I do, Alex. Because I'm in love with you."

She must expect me to tell her the same thing, but I can't do it. In my entire life, I have never spoken those three words to anyone. She said she's in love with me, not "I love you," but it feels the same to me. Am I in love with her? Just considering what the answer might be makes me itchy from head to toe.

Maybe she accepts me as-is for now, but sooner or later she will want more from me. And that will be the day I lose her.

Chapter Eight

Catriona

Living with Alex is the best thing that has ever happened to me. I don't even mind that he hasn't said he loves me, though I told him how I feel. Men don't like to deal with feelings, a fact I learned from watching my two older brothers deal with the lasses in their lives, beginning when they were teenagers. Aye, men have no clue how to handle romance. That's all right. I can wait for Alex to say those words because he shows me every day that he does love me.

Actions speak louder than words. That's how the saying goes, and I've decided to live by it.

When I ring my brother Lachlan six weeks after I moved in with Alex, I don't mention the man in my life. I've spoken to my sister Fiona in the meantime, but I didn't tell her either. I do let my family know I've changed addresses, and they don't ask why. They trust me. Sometimes I do feel guilty for keeping my relationship with Alex a secret, but I'm an adult, not a bairn. If I want to have this one thing for me and only me, without my family interfering or judging, then that's what I'll do. None of them suggest they might visit me in America. It's too far away and too expensive to fly here, and besides, they have their own lives. Moving here was always meant to be temporary, just until I get my PhD. My cousin Evan, who's almost done with his university studies, already knows more about computers than anyone I've ever met. So he helps us set up our computers to do video conferencing, which lets us see and hear each other.

Time flies by, but I love every minute of it. Sometimes I wish I could slow down the clock, just to have more time with Alex. But we have the rest of our lives. I won't get greedy and hope for more. I never ask him about his past. Am I a fool? Donnae care if I am. For the first time in my life, I have everything I need.

Six months after we moved in together, I get an offer I want to accept—but only if Alex doesn't mind. I'm excited to share the news with him, but I wait until we get home before I tell him. Alex had insisted on driving, and he might've crashed the car if I surprised him with my announcement. The second we walk into the loft and shut the door, I turn to stand in front of him, barring his way.

"What are you doing?" he asks. "If you want to shag before dinner, we should at least go into the living room to make use of the sofa. The entryway floor is marble, you know."

"I have something to tell you."

"Are you up the duff?"

Cannae help rolling my eyes at him. "No, I'm not pregnant."

He grasps my shoulders. "What is it, then?"

"I've been offered the chance to go on an excavation in Nevada."

"That's brilliant, Cat. Why do you look so stricken?"

"Because it means I'll be away for six weeks."

Alex pulls me into his arms and kisses my forehead. "I will miss you terribly, but I know how much this chance means to you. Go for it, love."

"I'll miss you too, Alex. Are you sure you don't mind?"

"You've wanted an opportunity like this for a long time, haven't you?" When I nod, he taps the tip of my nose. "I want you to do it. And maybe I could sneak onto the dig site in the dead of night to make love to you in your tent."

"We're staying in a motel."

"Even better. I can steal into your room."

"I'll have two roommates."

He tips his head back and makes a sarcastically pathetic noise. "I'll never survive."

I know he's joking, but I also know he will miss me—and I will miss him. Six weeks might pass quickly. Still, I'll think of him at least ten times a day. Leaving my home in Scotland hadn't been as difficult as spending six weeks away from Alex will be.

He drives me to the airport two weeks later, and he kisses me goodbye at the doors to the terminal.

As the plane takes off, I peer out the window as if I think I'll see Alex waving goodbye to me. Of course I can't spot him. But my heart hurts a wee bit when I realize I won't see him again for six weeks. The excavation takes my mind off Alex during the day, though not completely, and our nightly phone calls don't ease the stress of being away from home, away from him. Aye, the loft we share has become my home. I get every Sunday off, but that doesn't give me enough time to go back to Ballesteros and see Alex, though he offers to pay for my airline tickets. I know he has plenty of money. That's not the issue. I don't want to race back to Ballesteros just to spend a few hours with him. It wouldn't be relaxing, and I've got enough stress with the ongoing excavation.

But on my third Sunday in Nevada, Alex rings me on my mobile phone.

"What are you wearing, darling?" he asks instead of saying hello. "Please tell me you're having a naked pillow fight with your roommates."

"Afraid not, *gràidh*. They're both sleeping."

"But it's ten o'clock in the morning."

"You know how grueling an excavation can be."

He sighs. "Yes, but I never had a lie-in on my days off. And I had enough of field work while working on my PhD. That's why I became a professor."

"You are an amazing teacher. It's what you were meant to do."

"What I'm meant to do right now is shag you."

I stifle my laugh so I won't wake my roommates. "Are you suggesting phone sex?"

"No. I'm suggesting you get your arse to the Presidential Suite so I can make love to you in person."

"Presidential Suite? Where are you, Alex? I'm at an old motel on the outskirts of nowhere."

"That's where I am too, but I found better accommodations. Give me your address, and I shall pick you up in my chariot forthwith."

"Chariot? Your bum's oot the windae."

I recite the motel's address to him, and we say goodbye. How long will it take him to get here? I have no idea where his "presidential suite" is. This wee town has no luxury accommodations, which means Alex must be exaggerating. He likes to do that.

Ten minutes after our call ended, someone knocks on the door to my room. The two lasses I've been rooming with finally woke up and got dressed a wee while ago, though they keep yawning. I feel wide awake, not only because I got up early, but because I knew I'd see Alex any minute.

I swing the door open and smile. "Alex."

"Were you expecting some other bloke? I wouldn't mind your roommates joining us, but I won't share you with any other man."

From behind me, one of those roommates shouts, "Ooh! I'm in for a threesome with your super-hot boyfriend, Cat."

I glance over my shoulder at her. "No one shares Alex. He's mine."

The Brit in question smirks. "Rather possessive of me, aren't you?"

"Aye." Grabbing my purse, I push Alex backward with my body and shut the door. "You're mine, Dr. Thorne."

He slings an arm around my waist. "And you are mine, Catriona. By the way, I love it when you call me Dr. Thorne. It makes me very randy."

"Better get me to your 'presidential suite' fast, then."

"Not sure I can stand to wait that long."

When we reach his car, the one he hired at the airport, I realize I cannae wait either. So aye, we have a quick poke in the car. I straddle his lap and unzip his trousers, suddenly glad that I decided to wear a skirt and no knickers. After our quickie, Alex drives out to his "palatial accommodations" on the opposite side of town. Aye, he actually called this place palatial. I suppose it qualifies, if a body likes a worn-out mobile home with a creaky twin bed.

"This is your 'presidential suite'?" I ask.

"Yes. Nothing is too good for my girl. Shall I ring for room service?"

I pat his cheek. "You are the most adorable liar I've ever met."

He lifts my hand to his lips and kisses it. "I'm sorry I couldn't find better accommodations."

"Donnae worry, *gràidh*. I'm not a snob."

"You've called me that twice today. What does it mean?"

"Snob? It means—"

"The other word, love. The one that sounds like a different language."

"Oh, that." I lean in to whisper into his ear, "It means 'darling' in Gaelic. Does that fash you?"

"Well, I call you 'darling' in English, so I can't be annoyed because you say the same thing to me."

He doesn't mind what I said. Since he has never told me he loves me, I wondered if he might feel uncomfortable with endearments, especially since he knows I'm in love with him.

"I have champagne," he whispers into my ear. "Shall I pop the cork?"

"Yes."

He reaches under the bed and pulls out a bottle of sparkling white grape juice.

I laugh. "That's not champagne, Alex."

"Let's pretend it is. I couldn't find genuine bubbly anywhere in this charming hamlet, and I couldn't get real alcohol either. Apparently, this is a dry town."

"Donnae care. Let's pretend it is champagne."

He nuzzles my neck. "I'd love to pour this all over your body so I can lick it off."

"Only if I get to do the same thing to you."

For the rest of the day, we hide out in Alex's "presidential suite" and make believe the sparkling white grape juice we pour onto each other's bodies is really the most expensive champagne on earth. We laugh almost as often as we moan and gasp, and I lose count of how many times he makes me come. Sex with Alex is always more than just a path to orgasms. It's an experience.

Alex wants to throw out the empty bottle of sparkling grape juice. But I snatch it away. He tries to steal it from me while I dig in my purse to find my lipstick. It's a bonnie pink. I apply a thick coating to my mouth, then kiss the bottle's label, leaving my lip print.

"What's this?" he asks.

"A memento of our time in a luxurious hotel."

He smirks, then kisses me. And he takes the empty bottle with him when we leave.

Alex drives me back to the motel and kisses me again at the door to my room. He promises to come back every Sunday since he claims I'm the only thing that will sustain him and he will "die of starvation" if he can't devour me every weekend. I want to see him too, so I don't complain about his overblown claims.

During my last week in Nevada, I volunteer to drive to the nearby town of Fernley to get supplies—food and tools, not booze. As I'm walking out of the hardware store holding bags in each hand, I notice a man across the street just exiting a grocery store. His head is down, so I can't see his face, but something about his posture and gait seems familiar.

Then he lifts his head, revealing his profile, though it's partly in shadow.

Alex? No, it cannae be him. He's in New Mexico. My brief glimpse of the man as he climbs into a car parked along the street doesn't provide conclusive evidence. It can't be him. But a tingle swept down my spine when I saw that face. I rush across the street, but the man has driven away before I get there.

Was it Alex? Why would he keep it a secret that he came to Nevada? Maybe he means to surprise me.

I hurry back to the dig site and get to work, but I keep thinking about what I saw in Fernley. I glance at the road repeatedly during the rest of the day, hoping to see Alex driving up to surprise me. He doesn't. After a long day of work, we all head back to our motel. I ring Alex, but he doesn't answer. I take a shower, then try again. This time, he picks up.

"Good evening, Cat," he says. "Did you dig up any thrilling new finds?"

"No." I hesitate, afraid to hear his answer to the question I need to ask. But then I just do it. "Were you in Fernley, Nevada, today?"

"Fernley where? What are you on about?"

He sounds sincere in his confusion. As far as I know, Alex has never lied to me. He invents grandiose tales to entertain me, like when he called a dilapidated mobile home the "presidential suite." But he wouldn't outright lie. Would he? Of course not. I know Alex, and he's a good man.

"Why would you think I'm in Nevada?" he asks.

"I saw—I'm an eejit, that's all. Seeing mirages in the desert, I suppose."

"Your mirage was of me? I'm flattered."

We chat for a bit longer, then say goodbye so I can go to bed. A long day at the excavation site has left me jeeked. But as I'm falling asleep, one thought haunts me.

Did I imagine seeing a man who resembled Alex? Or is he hiding something from me?

Chapter Nine

Alex

Last night, I lied to Catriona. Well, it was more like I sort of obfuscated the truth. She must've suspected I had done that, though she held back from questioning me about it. I don't like keeping anything from Cat, but I cannot tell her the truth. Too much is at risk if I share everything with her. Maybe I should end our relationship and move away to a place where she can't find me.

Christ, what am I doing? Running away is not the answer. I haven't done anything illegal by taking a trip to Fernley without notifying Cat of my plans. Lying to her about it… That makes me feel like insects have burrowed deep under my skin. She isn't sure of what she saw. All I can do is hope the incident has faded from her memory by the time I fly to Nevada this weekend to see her.

If she remembers, she doesn't say anything. We enjoy a lovely Sunday together before I leave her.

When she finally comes home, everything goes back to normal. I've escaped by a hair this time, but I know one day she will realize the truth about me. This year, next year, or not until we're in our sixties. However long it takes, I know I can't avoid my past forever. Yes, I am a coward. A better man would tell her everything now.

It's too dangerous.

The months roll by, and soon even I've forgotten about that day in Fernley. All right, maybe I sort of think about it once in a while, but that doesn't mean I feel guilty. An important date arrives, taking my mind off whatever things I might have possibly worried about briefly now and then. I make plans to celebrate the occasion with Cat. I track her down in the university library. How do I know exactly where she is in this enormous building? I rang her mobile to find out. She didn't even ask why I wanted to know, or why I asked her to stay right where she is. She trusts me. I try not to consider the implications of that as I wend my way through the library to a corner on the lowest level which lies half underground. When I catch sight of her, I stop to admire the view.

Catriona stands on a wheeled ladder in an aisle between freestanding shelving units, stretching her body up in an attempt to reach the top shelf. She balances on her tiptoes with one arm outstretched. Her posture makes her shirt ride up, exposing her lower belly.

I come up behind her and palm her arse with both hands. "Careful, darling. You might fall."

Cat glances down at me and smiles. "Alex. What are you doing here?"

"Surprising you. Though I would've thought you'd guess my intentions when I rang to ask where precisely you were."

"I did wonder." She gives up on reaching whatever book she wanted and shimmies around to face me, leaning against the ladder. "Give me a hand?"

"Of course." I grasp her around the waist and pluck her off the ladder, setting her down on the carpeted floor. "No book is worth breaking your neck for."

She touches her lips to mine. "I wasn't going to break my neck. But you're so sweet to worry."

I slide an arm around her waist, pulling her snugly against me. "Do you know what today is?"

"Tuesday."

"Yes, but what else?"

She shrugs.

I cup her cheek in my hand. "It's our anniversary."

"Anniversary? Donnae understand."

"We met one year ago today." I reach behind my back to pluck an item out of my waistband. I hold up a single yellow rose for Cat to see. "This is for you, love. I've had you in my life for one full year, and I mean to demonstrate my gratitude for that fact."

"It's really been a year? Seems like just a few days ago when I saw you on that bench." She teases the hairs at my nape with her fingers. "I'm grateful for you too."

"We need to celebrate our anniversary. And I know exactly how to do that."

"Do you want to go back to the restaurant where we had our first date?"

"No." I back her up to the shelves, then place my mouth over her ear. "I mean to fuck you right here."

"In the library? We cannae do that, Alex."

"Of course we can." I reach into my trouser pocket and bring out a condom packet. "I'm fully prepared."

She glances side to side without moving her head. "We cannae."

I slide a hand down her thigh until I feel the hem of her skirt. "We can, and we will. Right now. Can you honestly tell me you don't want this as much as I do?"

Her breasts rise and fall as her breathing grows heavier. "I want this, but—"

"No thinking, Cat. Just give in to your desire." I push my hand under her skirt, gliding it up until I reach her knickers. Then I slip my fingers under the silky fabric to feel the hairs there. "Say yes, darling. Say it now."

She gasps when I tease her mound with my fingertips. "Yes, Alex, yes."

I grasp her knickers, tear them off, and lift them to my face to inhale the scent of her cream.

Cat starts breathing even harder, and she curls her fingers over the lip of one shelf.

"No more talking." I stuff her knickers in my pocket. She watches with rapt attention as I open the condom packet, unzip my trousers, and cover myself. "Time to make you come for me, love."

I lift her skirt up to her waist and grasp her thigh to hook it around my hip. She lashes her arms around my neck.

And I thrust into her.

Her eyes drift half-closed while I take her body in a slow and steady rhythm, the heat of her enveloping my cock. She lets her head fall back against the shelves even as she digs her fingers into my shoulders and wraps her thigh around me even more tightly. I take care not to push too hard. Why am I holding back? She loves it when I fuck her hard and fast and make her come so fiercely that she can't even shout my name. So what if the shelves might topple backward and spill books everywhere? I won't stop until she screams my name so loudly that even the patrons on the top floor can hear it.

I grip the shelf above her head with both hands and pound into her over and over, barely aware of the shelving unit creaking and the slapping of our bodies crashing together. Cat lashes both legs around me now, and her mouth falls open as if she's struggling not to cry out. I seal my mouth over hers, then shove a hand under her top and inside her bra to flick my thumb over the nipple, swallowing her cry.

Several books tumble off the shelves.

What if a book hits Cat on the head? Even while I keep thrusting into her wildly, I summon enough mental acuity to notice a table nearby. I pause in my thrusting only long enough to stagger to that table and lay her down on it. Since my cock is still nestled inside her, I need only start pumping again. She wraps her entire body around me, her face mashed to my neck, and I pummel her so powerfully that my ears ring and breaths bluster out of me in time with my movements.

The table wobbles. Something cracks, but my brain barely registers the sound.

Her inner muscles contract around me in strong, sensuous waves, and her body curls inward. Though her mouth gapes open, she can't make any sound except for a tiny, strangled gasp. I grip the table's edge above her head and slam into her a few more times. Then I collapse on top of her, almost wheezing while I try to regain control of my lungs. "Bloody hell, Cat. That was—"

The table tips sideways, then collapses.

Luckily, I had pulled my hands away from the table's edge before the thing crumpled to the floor. But I spring to my knees and frantically scan Cat's body. "Are you hurt?"

She seems a bit dazed, but she pushes up on her elbows and blinks up at me. "No, I'm fine. Did we actually break the table?"

"It must have been fragile to start with. But yes, I, ah, think we did break it." I survey her again. "Are you sure you haven't injured yourself?"

"Yes, Alex, I'm positive."

Offering her my hands, I help her up while I get to my feet too. She glances down at my groin, and her lips kink into a sexy expression that makes my cock twitch. "We knocked down books and destroyed a table. I can honestly say no other man has ever shagged me like that."

"Good. I never want to be boring."

"Might want to zip up your trousers before someone shows up to find out what happened down here."

Oh, that's why she stared at my cock. I zip up, then toss the condom into a nearby rubbish bin. "I might have just given you false expectations. I can't reasonably fuck you this way all the time, though I'd love to try."

She glances back at the table. "Aye, ye might have trouble topping this."

"Next time, I suppose I'll need to knock down an entire building to impress you."

Cat grasps my shirt and pulls me close. "Thank you for my anniversary gift."

I glance at the shelves and realize the rose I'd given her lies crushed under a large book. "Afraid your gift is now headed for the compost heap."

"That's not the gift I meant." She rubs her nose against mine. "You are the best thing that's ever happened to me. Thank you for being you, Alex."

What am I meant to say in response? She thinks I'm a gift. Catriona has given me more than I could ever explain, though I know I will never tell her that. I can't. Well, that's not quite true. I could, but I won't. Speaking the words feels like the most dangerous thing I could ever do. But in my thoughts, I can admit to the truth.

I am in love with Catriona MacTaggart.

Footsteps echo from elsewhere on this floor as someone rushes in our direction. A moment later, a young bloke comes around a corner and halts, gawping at the broken table. "What happened? I was in the microfiche room when I heard a crash."

The microfiche room is on the other side of this floor. Still, I'm surprised he could hear the crash. All these shelves seem like they would muffle that noise, but apparently not.

Cat stares at me, her eyes wide.

Time to do the one thing at which I never fail. I affect an air of cavalier disinterest as I wave a hand toward the table. "It must have been suffering from intense dry rot. The university really should take better care of its furniture."

"Dry rot?" the bloke says, his brows knitting together.

"Yes, that's right." I pull out my wallet and select several bills, then hand them to the confused young man. "This should cover the cost of replacing the table."

He flips through the bills, and his eyes bulge. "This is a thousand dollars."

"Take a bit for yourself, but save most of it for the library."

The young man bites his upper lip. "I'd better give it all to the library. I don't work here."

I pat his shoulder. "You are a rare upstanding citizen."

Then I clasp Cat's hand, leading her away.

Once we've exited the building, Cat halts and turns toward me. "You gave that boy a thousand dollars. For a table that probably cost fifty at most."

I shrug. "Money is not a problem for me. But you know that."

"Aye." She squints at me for a moment. That expression always means she's trying to figure me out. "I love you, Alex, but I don't think I'll ever understand you."

A wave of cold rushes through me. She had told me once that she's *in* love with me, but now she has proclaimed outright that she loves me. I know it's essentially the same thing. Still, I can't deny that her statement makes me uneasy. Things might be wonderful now, but eventually, my house of cards will fall.

But I won't think about that today.

I throw an arm around her shoulders and start walking. "Let's have lunch at our favorite restaurant. It is our anniversary, after all."

Cat grins—and my chest aches.

Chapter Ten

Catriona

For days after the library incident, I obsess over what happened and how Alex reacted when I said I love him. Aye, I'd told him almost a year ago that I'm in love with him, and I let him get away with not telling me how he feels. But now that I've said those three words, I thought he might say them back to me.

Why did I think that? Alex is Alex. He hasn't changed, and I need to accept that he might never express his feelings in words. He loves me, I know that. He proves that to me every day with his actions and the way he looks at me. Will I actually leave him if he never verbalizes his emotions? I've never met a man who wanted to do that. Maybe it doesn't matter what he says, only how he treats me.

No one has ever taken care of me the way Alex does. He always knows how to make me smile when I'm feeling anxious or stressed. And he remembered the one-year anniversary of the day we met. So I resolve to move on and enjoy my life with him, regardless of what he hasn't said.

I continue my studies in the meantime and secure a position as a teaching assistant for my second year at Ballesteros. Sometimes I even get to teach a class. Whenever that happens, I always notice a familiar face at the back of the room. Aye, Alex likes to sneak in to watch me. At first, that makes me feel nervous, but I get over that soon enough and begin to enjoy knowing he's there, supporting me just by observing. I peek into his classes too, though not as often as I'd like. My studies take up a lot of my time, especially since I've decided to begin mapping out what I'd like my dissertation to be, though I still have awhile to go before I reach that point in my doctoral program. Sneaking into Alex's classes helps me relax. He is mesmerizing, and I think every lass in the room has at least a wee crush on him.

Donnae blame them. I fell for him the day we met.

The months roll by, but I hardly notice the passing of time. My life is too full to worry about that. When I'm not on campus, I'm at home studying or having fun with Alex. When one of my professors asks if I'd like to do more field work at the site of newly discovered petroglyphs, I jump at the chance. An opportunity to study ancient rock art? Aye, that's a chance I can't pass up.

We're sitting on the sofa in our living room when I share the news. Alex clutches his chest and feigns having a heart attack, even falling over onto my lap.

"Are you done with your outlandish display?" I ask.

He doesn't sit up, not even when he smirks at me. "I think I'm paralyzed from the neck down. You'll need to stay home to care for me."

"I'll hire a nurse for you." I shake my head and pretend that I'm severely disappointed. "It's too bad you won't be able to have sex anymore. I'll have to find another man to satisfy my needs."

He springs upright, drags me into his body, and gazes straight into my eyes from inches away. "You don't need anyone else. No other man on earth could make love to you so thoroughly that the table you're shagging on breaks."

I brush my lips over his. "Are you sure you don't mind me leaving for two weeks?"

"Yes, darling, I'm sure. I'll miss you, but I never want to stop you from doing what makes you happy."

"I love archaeology, but you make me happier than anything else in the world."

He lifts my hand and kisses it. "It's the same for me, love."

I won't leave for Utah for another week, which gives me time to sit in on one of his classes the next afternoon. The subject for today is sexual imagery in the ancient world. He keeps the discussion academic and rather dry, probably because he worries he might get in trouble if he unleashes his naughty nature in a room full of fresh-faced undergraduates. I'd love to hear him give a real, no-holds-barred lecture on sexuality in the ancient world. But even this watered-down version is electrifying, thanks to the man giving the lecture. Alex Thorne is always a force to be reckoned with and the most unashamed person I've ever met. I think he would strip naked on the quad if he thought that would entertain his students and engage their minds.

Once all the students have filed out of the room, Alex approaches me. "Did you enjoy the show, Cat?"

"Aye, it was wonderful. I think you made all the female students blush. I'm dead sure they all want to shag you."

"The only woman I want is you."

I might be blushing now too. Donnae know why, but every time Alex says something like that, I feel like a silly schoolgirl again.

We walk out of the building while holding hands, then find our favorite bench on the quad so we can discuss my upcoming trip. We agree that while I'm away in Utah, Alex and I will talk on the phone at least three times a day. He suggests we could try phone sex to avoid "the tragedy of not actually fucking each other for two weeks." I feel strange about the prospect of doing that. It's not real sex. We would masturbate while listening to each other over the phone. Besides, I'll be sharing a room with another student, so we wouldn't have privacy.

Alex expresses his disappointment with sarcasm, of course, but I know he doesn't really mind. That's one of his best qualities—his desire to make me happy, even if that means he doesn't get exactly what he wants. I wish I could make him happy too. And aye, I've been thinking of ways I can make it up to him once I get home. My plans involve lots of sex, of course, but also plenty of kissing and cuddling. Alex loves to make cheeky comments about snuggling, but I know he secretly loves it.

On the last day before I fly to Utah, I'm sitting on our bench waiting for Alex. He often gets waylaid by students after class, most of whom want to talk about their studies. A few of the lasses just like to bat their eyelashes at him. I've never been jealous. I know he loves me, and he has no interest in other women. He doesn't even glance at buxom blondes who wear skimpy clothes.

While I wait, I admire the clear blue sky and the birds flying past overhead.

A group of students wander over to my bench—three lads and two lasses. One lad steps closer to me and leans in to study my face. "You're Dr. Thorne's girl, aren't you? Everybody knows about you two."

"If you know who I am, why did you ask?"

He shrugs and sits down at the opposite end of the bench, draping an arm over its back. His fingers are inches away from my shoulder. "I love Irish chicks."

"I'm Scottish."

"Same diff." He smiles in a way he probably thinks is charming, but I think he looks like a moron. "Why do you want to date a British guy? He's a dick, that's what I hear. Let me take you out tonight, and I'll show you what a red-blooded American can do."

"Thank you for the offer, but my social calendar is full."

"Social calendar?" he says with a laugh. "Damn, the way you say that makes me so hot for you."

"I feel chilly for you."

"Catriona, darling, you should've told me you invited your harem." Alex walks up to the bench and offers me his hand. He holds a picnic basket in his other hand. "I would've brought more food. Group sex always leaves me famished."

I accept Alex's hand, rising from the bench.

The American scunner stands up too and sneers at Alex. "Dude, I don't get naked with other guys."

"Neither do I, so we're even." Alex waves a hand in a negligent gesture. "Toddle off to your nursery. I'm sure it's time for your next bottle feeding."

"You really think you're hot shit, don't you? Nobody here is impressed, sissy boy."

Alex chuckles. "I've been called much worse than that."

"I bet you have." The scunner moves closer, and his friends edge nearer too. "I can take you anytime, anywhere."

"Can you?" Alex sets down the picnic basket and steps to the side, drawing out a distance between us. "Let's make a wager on that."

"You're on. What are the stakes?"

Alex pulls a quarter out of his pocket and holds it up between his thumb and forefinger. "If you can take this coin from me, I'll let you have Catriona."

He won't actually give me to the eejit. Whatever Alex means to do, he's dead sure he can pull it off. And I trust him. Besides, I never agreed to this wager, so I can skelp the laddie if he wins. Aye, that means I'll slug him. It helps to grow up with three brothers. They taught me how to throw a punch.

"On the count of three," Alex tells the scunner, "you grab the coin. One, two, three."

The laddie lunges for Alex, but the Brit dodges the American deftly. The eejit tries three times, but he can't catch Alex. So he tries to ram his head into Alex's gut, but the Brit sidesteps him again. The lad trips and falls down on the concrete path.

"I'll report you to the campus police," the scunner snarls as he struggles to his feet. "That's assault."

"No, it's not," Alex says while tossing the coin and catching it in his palm. "I never laid a finger on you. Your clumsiness is hardly my fault."

"I want a rematch."

"Well, if you insist." Alex tucks the coin into his trouser pocket. "Try to get that quarter now."

The laddie runs toward the Brit and shoves his hand into Alex's pocket, clearly trying to retrieve the coin. He digs around in there as if he can't quite find the quarter. Finally, the laddie gives up, throws his arms in the air, and lets out a frustrated noise. "You cheated somehow. It's not in your pocket."

"I never said it was." Alex opens his hand, palm up, revealing the coin. "You assumed that's what I meant when I told you to try to get that quarter."

The scunner bares his gritted teeth. "You slimy—"

"Uh-uh-uh. I never assaulted you. But I'm afraid all these witnesses watched you assault me and sexually harass me."

"I never touched your dick."

"You were rooting about in my trousers."

"Because you said—Gah! You're one sick, twisted piece of work."

Alex tosses the coin to the laddie. "Here's your consolation prize. Now toddle back to your wet nurse. A twat like you shouldn't try it on with a sophisticated woman."

Did he just call me sophisticated? No one has ever referred to me that way before. I like it.

The "twat" makes a petulant face, then stalks away with his mates trailing after him. The crowd disperses quickly now that the excitement has ended.

Alex takes my hand, holding it more firmly than usual. "Are you all right, love?"

"I'm fine. You know how to handle a scunner. I'm impressed."

He winces the slightest bit. "It's a skill I learned out of necessity."

I want to ask him what that means, but he doesn't like to discuss his past. Am I a fool for not demanding he tell me everything? Maybe that's why I've never told my family about

Alex. Sometimes I wonder if, deep down, I know our relationship won't last forever.

The next day, Alex drives me to the airport and kisses me goodbye. Aye, I'll miss him.

As for how long we might last… I'll think about that another time.

Chapter Eleven

Alex

Catriona flew to Utah six days ago, and I've spent the entire week teaching classes while on autopilot and making appropriate noises while students tell me their problems during my office hours. I barely notice anything they say. I can't remember what topics I discussed in my lectures. All my mind will let me think about is Cat. Friday evening, I can't take it anymore. I get on a plane and fly to Salt Lake City, Utah. Luckily, I manage to secure a suite at the most expensive hotel in the city, which isn't expensive by my standards. Catriona will think it is. But she deserves a plush mattress—to sleep on and to shag on.

I ring her from the suite.

She answers with a sleepy hello.

"Been working hard?" I say. "Well, it's a good thing I've come to whisk you away to my palace. Your servant shall attend to your every need and desire."

"Alex? What are you talking about?"

"I'm here in Salt Lake City."

"Here?" She sounds more awake now. "Where? We're staying at a tiny motel on the south side of town."

"Give me the motel's name, and I'll find it. Don't eat anything because I mean to spoil you with five-star room service."

"You don't need to do that."

"Of course I do. Now give me that address."

She recites it for me, and we say goodbye. Half an hour later, I pull into the car park at the rundown little establishment where the archaeology team has taken up residence. If I'd known what sort of hovel she'd been staying at, I would've insisted on booking her a suite for the duration. She wouldn't have let me, though. Cat is bloody-minded when it comes to letting me spoil her.

Tonight, she will be treated like a princess—whether she likes it or not.

When I knock on the door to her room, a blonde with spiky hair and a nose ring opens it. Her eyes widen, and she peruses my entire body before speaking. "Who are you? And how can I get some of what you're selling?"

"I'm here for Catriona."

The girl sighs. "Oh well. It figures a hot guy wouldn't knock on the door for me." She twists her head around to shout, "Cat! Your boyfriend is here."

Catriona appears behind the spiky-haired girl and tells her, "I'll be gone until Monday morning."

"Have fun." The girl winks at me. "Don't work her too hard, hon."

Since I have no response to that, I clasp Catriona's hand and lead her to the car I hired at the airport. It's a BMW sports car, but Cat doesn't comment on my choice of vehicle. She lifts her brows a touch, that's all. During the drive back to my hotel, she fills me in on what happened today during the team's investigation of the newly found petroglyphs. I always love listening to her talk, mostly because she has the sexiest voice, but also because I enjoy her enthusiasm. I don't think I've ever gotten as excited about archaeology as she does.

Every time she smiles, I smile too. And every time she laughs, I do the same.

When we arrive at the hotel, I park the car and rush to get to the passenger door before she can open it herself. Cat always kisses my cheek when I do that. She brought a small bag, so I carry that for her. She kisses my cheek again. But when we reach my suite, all she seems capable of doing is gawping and turning in circles.

"Is something wrong?" I ask.

She stops twirling and stares at me blankly for a moment. Then she blinks rapidly. At last, she looks at me and shakes her head. "You weren't joking when you called this your palace."

"It's a hotel suite, not the residence of a king."

"Might as well be that. This is even more posh and expensive than our loft. It might be bigger too."

"Try the bed. You'll love it."

She lies down atop the covers and links her hands above her head. Her eyes drift shut, and a sensual smile curves her lips. "You need to shag me on this bed right now, Alex."

"What about dinner?"

"Sex first." She opens her eyes and stretches her entire body, sighing with contentment. "Undress me, Alex. You know I love it when you do that."

I tug my shirt out of my waistband and begin unbuttoning it. "Writhe around a bit more, darling. I love watching you move."

She stretches her arms above her head and wriggles her hips.

By the time I've shed my clothes, my cock is hard as steel. Maybe I shouldn't have encouraged her to writhe about like an erotic serpent, because I don't know if I can wait more than thirty seconds to fuck her. Self-control is my forte, though, and I strip her swiftly. Then I take my time getting her ready for me, gorging myself on her cream until she comes for me like a dew-drenched flower blooming in my hands. We make love until we're too knackered to have another go, then we order room service. Cat informs she is "fair starved," so I choose a wide selection of dishes and desserts for us. After that, we can't shag again. Our bellies are too full. Instead, we crawl under the covers and sleep.

The next day, we stay in the suite to talk and shag. I won't see Cat again for another week, when she will finally come home. I'd survived six weeks away from her last year, so two weeks shouldn't seem like a terrible trial, but it does. Though I don't tell Catriona, on my way home I make a detour to Fernley to visit the only two people in the world who know all the things Cat wants me to tell her. She accepted not knowing, but I doubt she will go on accepting the secrecy forever.

Maybe that's why I need to be with her as much as possible.

A week later, I pick her up at the airport. Then I do something I've never done before, though I can't explain why I need to do it. I wait at the curb, leaning against the car, and the instant she walks out of the terminal, I pull her close for a deep, hot kiss. I don't give a stuff that everyone must be staring at us. When I pull away, Cat seems dazed.

I brush stray hairs away from her cheek. "Welcome home, love."

"Alex, I..." She glances around with a guilty expression. "You shouldn't do that in public."

"Why not? I missed you."

Her lips curl into an adorable smile. "I missed you too."

"I've decided you are forbidden from going anywhere without me ever again, not even to the grocery store." I open the passenger door and hold her hand while she climbs inside. "I won't survive another separation."

Can't believe I said that. Cat seems shocked too.

I pretend I haven't just confessed in the most embarrassing way and hurry to the driver's door. As I navigate the airport road, I avoid glancing at Catriona. Well, I try to do that. But my eyes insist on glancing her way.

She's smiling.

"We've reached another milestone," I say. "Today it's been exactly one year and ten months since we moved in together."

"That long? It feels like yesterday."

"How should we celebrate? I vote for sex."

She laughs. "You always vote for sex. If I asked what you want to eat for dinner, you'd say let's have a poke instead."

"Oh no, I would never say 'have a poke.' I would've told you let's shag, or possibly let's get a leg over."

"A man who's an expert on ancient sexual practices can do better than that."

"Is that a challenge?" I throw her a sideways smirk. "When we get home, I'll read you excerpts from a medieval collection called *The Decameron*. One of my favorite stories concerns randy nuns who each have their way with one young bloke. He must've been completely knackered but very happy after that."

"You should read me those stories. After dinner."

I sigh with no small amount of sarcasm. "Yes, I will feed you first."

"Thank you, Alex."

"But I will need to feast on you after."

She throws her head back and laughs so boisterously that, whilst admiring her joyful expression, I take my eyes off the road for a moment too long. A horn blares. I veer the car back into our lane just in time.

And Cat laughs again.

We do eat first, then shag between my recitations of bawdy medieval literature. By the time we finish, it's after midnight. We both need to get up early in the morning, but neither of us minds the lack of sufficient sleep. Memories of last night keep me awake all day.

Later in the week, I run a secret errand. Catriona has gone to the library to do research for the potential topic of her dissertation, so I seize the chance to do a bit of shopping on my own. Impulsive purchases are not my strong suit, but I felt inspired this afternoon, and since I had no classes after four o'clock, I decided to just do it.

I visit a jewelry store.

The clerk helps me choose two items. The first is a pair of sapphire earrings that will complement Cat's eyes. I couldn't find a pair with stones as pale as her irises, but I chose the lightest blue available. The stones are surrounded by white gold. She will look lovely in these earrings, but that isn't the most important thing I wanted to buy today. I keep the second item in its box and slip it into my trouser pocket as I walk out of the store—until I realize the box creates a visible shape in my pocket. So I pull it out and remove the ring, stashing that in my pocket instead. Yes, it's a diamond ring. The glittering stone rests in a cradle of much smaller stones, all of them surrounded by white gold.

Tonight, I am going to propose to Cat.

I ring Cat on her mobile to ask when she might be home. She assures me she'll be done at the library in an hour, then she will come straight home. That leaves me with enough time to do what I need to do. She will say yes. Won't she? Of course she will. I set about making our lavish meal and creating the proper atmosphere for a proposal, which means candlelight and soft, sensual music, as well as roses in a glass vase and a lace tablecloth that I bought on my way back from the jewelry store. I also change my clothes. A suit without the tie seems more appropriate than the T-shirt and khaki trousers I'd been wearing.

Catriona arrives moments after I've finished the preparation. She hurries into the house while staring down into her purse as if she's hunting for something.

I clear my throat.

She freezes and glances up. "Alex, what is all this?"

"Dinner. It's a special occasion."

"What sort of occasion?"

I pull out a chair and gesture toward it. "Have a seat, and you'll find out."

Ringing emanates from her purse. She digs her mobile out and answers it. "Lachlan?"

Her brother isn't supposed to know about me, but I can't help wondering if fate has given him a nudge. Either that or I'm cursed. Why else would her brother call tonight? She doesn't speak to her family every day.

"Oh, aye," she says to Lachlan. "Well, I should speak to Jamie first. She's a teenager, and everything seems like a catastrophe at that age."

This does not sound promising, not for my proposal plans.

Cat disconnects the call and gives me a sheepish look. "I'm sorry, Alex. The dinner you've made looks wonderful, but I need to ring my sister Jamie. Her boyfriend just broke up with her. Threw her over for another girl. She won't stop crying, and she won't speak to anyone, not even our sister Fiona. Lachlan wants me to try to calm Jamie down."

"You should do that, then. I'll keep the food warm."

"This might take hours, Alex. Go ahead and eat."

Whilst she heads into the bedroom, I make a plate of food for her and deliver it to her. She gives me a grateful smile. I eat alone in the living room. By the time her call to Jamie ends, we both want nothing more than to go to sleep. I don't ask her to marry me. I don't even tell her about the ring. I do give her the earrings, which she loves, but I've apparently lost my nerve when it comes to popping that question. Maybe her sister's romantic problems are a sign that I shouldn't propose to Cat. I don't do it the next day or the day after that, not a week later either. I have lost my nerve, haven't I? That has never happened to me before. But then, I've never loved any woman except for Catriona MacTaggart.

And I still haven't told her that either.

Chapter Twelve

Catriona

Alex has been behaving strangely ever since last night, when I came home to find he had cooked a big dinner for us. He said he understood why I needed to talk to my sister, and he gave me the beautiful earrings he'd bought as a not-quite anniversary gift. When I opened the box and saw the light-blue sapphire stones, I couldn't believe what he'd done. Expensive earrings? There's no such thing as a year and ten months anniversary, but I didn't tell Alex that. For some reason, he wanted to turn a pseudo-event into a real one, and he was clearly disappointed when that didn't happen.

This morning, I wake up alone in our bed. After quickly dressing, I rush into the living room to look for Alex. He's in the kitchen making tea, it looks like, staring down at two cups as he fills them.

He lifts his head when I approach the island and smiles tightly. "Good morning, Catriona."

"Aye, good morning, Alex. I'm sorry about last night."

"You have already apologized several times. There's no need for more." He hands me a cup. "I ate earlier, but I'd be happy to make something for you."

"I can do that myself." Alex always waits to have breakfast with me. The fact that he didn't today, coupled with his tight expression, proves that he's not himself this morning. "Are you sure you aren't upset about last night? I know you had a gourmet meal planned for us—"

"Not gourmet. Just food."

"But Alex—"

"I am fine, Cat. Stop worrying." He strides over to the sofa and sits down, taking a sip of his tea. "I let you have a bit of a lie-in, but you should eat quickly or you'll miss your nine o'clock class."

My gaze darts to the clock on the microwave oven. *"Mhac na galla.* I didn't realize how late it was."

After a quick breakfast, I gulp down the last of my tea and grab my rucksack, then race out to the car. Alex is already in the driver's seat with his hands firmly gripping the wheel. He stares straight ahead, only glancing at me sideways. The second I've got my seatbelt done up, he backs out of the driveway and onto the road. We don't speak in the car. And when we arrive at the campus, Alex gives me a quick peck on the cheek before he marches off to his office.

I go to class, but I have trouble concentrating. Why is Alex in such a mood? He doesn't seem angry. I almost think he's embarrassed or ashamed. Alex is the most confident man I've ever met, so I cannae imagine what might upset him this way. We have lunch together, and he seems more relaxed then. I hesitate to ask him about last night and this morning, but by the time we're done eating, I can't wait any longer.

So I set down my water bottle and face him. "I know you said you didn't mind that I talked to Jamie instead of having dinner with you last night. But I feel like I have hurt you by doing that."

"Not hurt." He wriggles on the bench and avoids looking at me. "I was disappointed. You see, I had planned—Well, it was nothing, really."

"Please tell me, Alex."

His fingers curl into his thighs. He still won't look at me. "I had an idea, but I realized later that it was just as well my plans didn't work out."

"What plans? Dinner? I donnae understand why it was just as well that didn't happen."

"Not dinner." He shoves a hand into his hair and sighs. "Can we forget about last night? I'd rather move on."

I've lived with Alex for almost two years, and I know that once he decides a topic is closed, I can't convince him to reopen it. Aye, I knew when I started dating him that he had secrets he would never share with me. I accepted that because I believed the present and future mattered more than the past. Was I an eejit to believe that?

Alex rises and tosses the remnants of his lunch into a nearby trash bin. "I'll meet you at the car after your last class."

He doesn't even kiss me goodbye. He just walks away.

In a situation like this, I would normally ring one of my sisters to talk about it. I can't do that. Once I resolved to keep our relationship a secret, at least from my family, I shut that door for good.

After my last class, I step out into the corridor, prepared to head for the faculty car park. But Alex is there in the hall, leaning against the wall.

He smiles and takes my hand. "Shall we go, darling? I'm famished, so I thought we might stop at our favorite bakery for a decadent snack."

Aye, he has suddenly reverted to his usual self. And I feel like a crash test dummy that just got flung through a windshield.

"I'm glad you're in a better mood," I say as we walk down the corridor. "But it seems to have happened very fast."

"Never mind last night or this morning." He slings an arm around my shoulders and aims his patented charming smile at me, the one that always makes me forget everything except how much I love him. "I prefer to focus on right now, with you."

Maybe I should question him, but he starts telling me humorous stories about his students, and I love listening to him describe those incidents. Alex is a consummate storyteller—and a consummate seducer. Whether he uses his charms to enthrall students during a lecture or to make love to me, I've never been able to resist him when he's like this.

We visit the bakery and enjoy a selection of pastries chosen by Alex. When I bite into a raspberry Danish, and a bit of the filling sticks on my lips, Alex leans over to drag his tongue across my mouth and remove the jam. Then he leans in more to whisper into my ear, "We have caramel syrup at home. I'd love to drizzle that over your skin and lick it off slowly."

Aye, we hurry home to do that.

Though I've mostly set my worries aside, in the back of my mind, a question niggles at me. How much do I really know about Alex? Until recently, I would've answered that question with another one. How much can anyone really know about their partner? But now... I don't know what to think about anything.

A few days later, I manage to surprise Alex. He would never tell me when his birthday was, but this year, I resolve to find out. If he won't tell me, I will discover the truth on my own. But I'm not a private investigator. I don't need to be, since Alex leaves his wallet on the nightstand when we go to bed. When I wake in the middle of night, I take his wallet and tiptoe into the living room so I can turn on a lamp. Then I find his driving license.

His birthday was three weeks ago.

It might be a wee bit late, but I mean to celebrate that occasion. In the morning, I get up before Alex and start baking. By the time he walks into the living room, I've completed my mission.

Alex stops halfway to the kitchen island. "What are you doing over there? It doesn't smell like breakfast."

"Oh, I made that too. But I also baked something just for you." I raise the plate that holds the layer cake I made. "Happy birthday, Alex."

"Today is not my birthday."

"I know. But I missed the actual day because you would never tell me when it was."

"That's because I don't celebrate it."

I set the cake down and light the candles, then carry it over to him. "Make a wish and blow out your candles."

He eyes the cake with suspicion while the flames flicker and wax dribbles down toward the icing. "This is important to you."

"Aye. And to you, whether you realize it or not. You insisted on celebrating my birthdays, and you gave me presents too." I hold the cake closer to him. "The candles will melt if you don't blow them out."

He sucks in a breath and puckers his lips.

"Make a wish too, Alex. Please, for me."

He rolls his eyes and blows out the candles. "Aren't you going to ask what I wished for?"

"No, of course not. That's private. I never told you what I wished for either." I place the cake on the island. "Time to cut a slice and eat it. Sorry I don't have a gift for you."

"No need for trinkets. You are the only gift I need."

Alex cuts two slices of cake, and we eat that before we have breakfast. While we're cleaning up after our impromptu celebration, I get curious. "You say you don't like birthday parties and presents, but you gave me both of those last year and this year."

"That's different. You should celebrate your birthday. It's a happy occasion for you and your family."

"But not for you."

"No." He finishes putting the last of the plates into the dishwasher. "Besides, I only gave you a bottle of Scottish whisky. It wasn't even an expensive brand."

"It was Talisker, my brother Lachlan's favorite. I mentioned that to you, but I never expected you'd buy me a bottle of single-malt Scotch whisky direct from the Isle of Skye."

"Well, I thought it might make you feel less homesick."

"You are my home, Alex. I never feel sad about leaving Scotland."

He stares at me for a moment, then clears his throat. "We should get going or you'll be late for class."

We don't discuss birthdays or gifts anymore. Everything goes back to normal, though we do have cake for dessert three evenings in a row.

One day, Alex and I are browsing the shops in downtown Ballesteros when a strange thing happens. He has just ducked into a novelty store after announcing he needs to take care of a "secret errand." Those were his exact words. He might not like birthdays, but he loves surprising me with wee gifts. So I sit down on a bench near the curb and watch the traffic go by while I wait for Alex.

A woman sits down at the opposite end of the bench. I recognize her, though I only saw her once before. This is the woman Alex had a poke with on the night before he met me. What does she want now?

"Hey, Catriona," she says, though she seems unsure of how to pronounce my name. "Glad we bumped into each other again."

"I have nothing to say to you."

"Oh, I don't want to have a conversation. Where is Alex, anyway?"

"How do you know our names? We never told you."

She smiles. "I have connections, hon. That time when I saw Alex on the street, he turned me down when I offered him another chance to screw me. But I bumped into another guy, somebody who was more than happy to get tangled in the sheets with me, no strings attached."

"Is there a point to your story? I donnae care if you shag every man in the city."

"Here comes the point, hon." She sidles a wee bit closer. "The man I screwed in my hotel room that day turned out to be powerful. He hooked me up with a sweet bachelorette pad, and we've been doing the nasty twice a week ever since."

I've had enough of this. I rise and smooth my blouse.

"Oh, you can't go yet," she says. "Sit down, Catriona. My name is Gloria Harris, by the way. We should be on a first-name basis considering what I want from you."

"Which is what?"

"Alex. I want to fuck him again, on a regular basis. My new lover is good, but Alex was better."

"You are off your head."

Just as she opens her mouth to speak again, Alex strides out of the shop carrying a small bag. He halts beside me and narrows his gaze on Gloria. "What are you doing here?"

"Having a girl chat with Catriona."

"Bugger off. Neither of us has anything to say to you."

"Come on, baby—"

"Leave now," he says in the nastiest tone I've ever heard. "Go, or I will force you to do it."

Gloria raises her hands. "Okay, okay. I'll go. But we'll be seeing each other again."

She ambles down the pavement and eventually disappears from our view.

"What did that slag say to you?" Alex asks.

"That she lives here now, and she has a powerful lover. Oh, and she wants to shag you."

He grunts. "Don't worry about her. She is clearly a very unhappy woman." He offers me the bag he'd been carrying. "Here's your surprise."

I pull out the items inside the bag—two teddy bears, a boy and a girl. The girl is dressed in a white T-shirt that has the Scottish flag printed on it while the boy's shirt features the British flag. I can't help laughing. "Thank you, Alex. You are so sweet."

He hooks an arm around my waist. "If ever I'm not here to cuddle with you, these bears will fill in for me."

I kiss his cheek. "This was very thoughtful."

As we head for home, I wonder about his statement. Why wouldn't he always be here with me? He must've meant that if I go on another excavation, or if he goes on a trip, I can use the bears as a fuzzy surrogate.

Aye, that must be what he meant. Isn't it?

Chapter Thirteen

Alex

Catriona seemed puzzled when I gave her two teddy bears, and I can't blame her for that reaction. Why did I do it? Stuffed animals to stand in for me. It's ridiculous. Yet lately, I keep feeling like my time with her is limited and I need to appreciate every moment. Seeing that stupid woman again did not help matters. Cat is even more confused by her encounter with the tart I fucked once than she is by the gift of stuffed animals. I have no clue what that woman wants, though I'm positive it isn't just another shag with me.

On the way home, Cat told me the woman calls herself Gloria Harris. Well, if that's her real name, I can find her—and find out what the bloody hell she wants. I need to know more about the woman who seems determined to cock up my life.

After Catriona falls asleep that night, I sneak into the living room to search the internet for some clue about who Gloria Harris is. The woman claims to have a powerful new lover, but that might be bollocks. I refuse to believe Gloria simply wants my body. She is up to something, and I doubt it's a good thing. So I use my admittedly mediocre internet skills to hunt for answers. My first search nets me thousands of women with the same name. *Bugger me.* This will take years. I can't risk hiring a private investigator. If Cat found out, she would want to know why I'm paranoid about a virtual stranger harassing us. I told her after the most recent encounter that I'm sure it's nothing and she shouldn't worry.

Cat believed me. She trusts me. Whether she should… Well, I'll worry about that later.

I trust no one, with only three exceptions including Catriona.

Since I must do this alone and in secret, I go back to bed and pretend to sleep. Maybe I do catch a bit of sleep, but not enough. I put on a good show for Cat, pretending that I'm well-rested and carefree. I even suggest we eat lunch at a restaurant instead of bringing our own food and having our meal on our favorite bench. After that, I drop Catriona off on campus, telling her I need to run a few errands. It's to do with my classes, of course. Now I'm outright lying to her. I swore to myself I would never do that, but I have no choice. If Gloria turns out to be just a woman who has a crush on me, I'll never need to tell Cat about any of this. It won't matter that I lied. The untruths will evaporate.

Yes, I've spent a lifetime learning how to con other people. Now I'm doing it to myself.

Catriona told me yesterday that Gloria claimed to have a "bachelorette pad" paid for by her new lover. She was wearing what looked like designer clothing, as well as large diamond earrings and a large emerald ring. If her lover paid for those items too, which seems likely, then I should be able to figure out where she lives. It would be a posh flat or a house. Any man who gives a woman designer clothes wouldn't set her up in a tenement. This town doesn't have many clothing stores, which means it shouldn't take me long to figure out where she bought her wardrobe and where she lives. I remember what Gloria was wearing yesterday, which gives me enough information to get started on my search.

I visit several shops, asking similar questions about the items they sell, taking care not to sound too interested. I tell the store clerks that my girlfriend loved an outfit that one of her mates bought and she wants to find something by the same designer. Then I describe Gloria's ensemble. After striking out four times, I finally hit a home run.

And I don't even like baseball.

The clerk in the fifth shop remembers Gloria's outfit and the woman herself. Apparently, she loves a particular designer, Amadeo Gaspari, whose clothing is only sold in this store. The bloke lives in a nearby town and attended Ballesteros University. I learn the name of the clerk, Angelina, and chat her up—though I'm careful not to give her the impression I have any sexual interest in her. I walk a very fine line with sweet little Angelina. Maybe that's why I feel slightly nauseous after my conversation with her.

But I get the information I need.

No, Angelina does not provide that information. Not directly. After browsing the items designed by Amadeo Gaspari, I ask Angelina if the shop has any more of his creations that haven't been brought out for display yet. She disappears into a back room to check.

I take the opportunity to investigate. Leaning over the counter, I snatch up what looks like a logbook of customers and purchases. While I keep half an eye on the door to the back room, I skim the logbook in hopes of discovering the information I need. Just when I think I've struck out—and yes, I need to give up on the ruddy baseball metaphor—I finally see a name I recognize.

Gloria Harris.

The logbook includes her home address and phone number. I grab a flyer from a stack on the counter, flip it over to the blank backside, and scrawl Gloria's contact information on it. Just as I tuck the folded paper into my pocket, Angelina returns. She couldn't find anything in the back room. I thank her and leave.

Now that I have Gloria's address, I have no idea what I meant to do with it. Spy on her? Confront the woman? For the moment, I can't do anything. I need to go back to the campus to pick up Catriona and go home. My investigation will need to wait until tomorrow.

That night, as we're settling in for bed, Cat snuggles up to me and traces circles on my bare chest with her delicate fingertips. "Let's make love, Alex."

Considering what I've been doing today—deceiving her, spying on a stranger, playing detective—I know I can't get aroused, not even for Cat. I'm tired and on edge.

"What's wrong?" she asks. "You seem anxious."

"No, I'm tired after grading papers all afternoon."

Another deception. Never before have I wished I weren't so good at conning people. If she caught me in a lie, at least my secret mission would be out in the open, and I wouldn't need to obfuscate the truth anymore. But I can't make myself confess, and she trusts me too much to suspect anything.

Cat crawls under the covers and closes her eyes. "Good night, Alex."

"Good night, love."

Another night with little sleep leaves me even more on edge in the morning. But I do what I must, relying on skills I thought I'd left in the past, and convince her I feel right as rain today. I want to ask my teaching assistant to handle my classes, but Catriona might stop in at my office to see me. She likes to do that whenever she has time. So I slog my way through topics I normally love to discuss, biding my time until I can sneak away to continue my espionage mission.

Lunch with Cat tests my acting skills, but I don't think she noticed anything amiss. Christ, she really does trust me without reservations. I don't deserve her faith, but I can't make myself push her away.

At least I get one bit of luck. Gloria's house lies on the outskirts of town, and trees screen it from the view of nearby homes. The lot has a large yard which provides even more camouflage thanks to more trees lining either side of the property. All of that means I can easily spy on her. I park my car a block away, on a side street, and skulk onto Gloria's property. I'd worn dark clothes today, knowing I would be doing this.

Catriona complimented me on my clothing. She thinks it's "dead sexy." And her statement made me feel like even more of a bastard.

But I'm doing this for her.

No, I'm not sure even I believe that anymore. I don't want Gloria anywhere near Cat ever again, partly because the woman upsets her, but mostly because I don't want her telling my girlfriend about all the things I did with her. Gloria's vague threats might mean nothing. She could simply enjoy causing trouble.

Just as I'm skulking around the house from behind, approaching the front corner, a nondescript four-door car pulls into the driveway. The visitor parks right behind what I take for Gloria's vehicle. The cherry-red convertible looks like a luxury model, though I know little about cars other than how to buy and drive one.

A man steps out of the other car.

I pull out my mobile phone and take a picture of the gent as he saunters up to the front door, then brings out a key to let himself in. I approach the living room window and peer inside, hoping for a glimpse of the man and Gloria. I don't need to wait long. The couple walks into the living room and sits down on the sofa. The house appears to be furnished in style, probably with designer furniture to match Gloria's designer clothes and her expensive car.

The man pulls Gloria into his arms and kisses her passionately.

He is definitely her new lover. I snap a few pictures of them snogging, then sneak around the front of the house to capture an image of the license plate on the man's car. I also photograph Gloria's license plate. With this information, maybe I can figure out who the geezer is.

I mean to head back to my car, but I need to pass by Gloria's house to do that. As I slink away, movement catches my eye in a different room, and I sidle up to the window. Gloria and her lover are in bed. Naked. Fucking on top of the sheets as if they couldn't wait even to pull the covers back before they started shagging. Though I feel like a ruddy voyeur, I take several pictures of the couple in flagrante. They go at it like animals. Gloria hadn't been quite that passionate with me, a fact for which I am grateful. Behaving like a rutting stag does not appeal to me.

Now that I have some evidence, I return to my car and drive back to the campus to pick up Cat. After dinner, I tell her I need to work on lesson plans for next week, which is true, but that's not the main reason I need time alone. I don't get my wish, though. Cat insists on watching the telly while I sit on the sofa with my computer on my lap. I glance up and find her smiling at me, the expression soft and affectionate.

Bile rises into my throat. I grab my water glass from the table and guzzle the entire contents.

With the woman I love nearby, I plug my mobile into the computer and download the pictures I took today. Then I find a website that will let me search for public information easily, just by paying a fee. My search gives me what I wanted to know—the name of the man who owns Gloria's house. He is Darnell Miller, and he serves as the chief of police in Ballesteros. That means he does have influence in the community, though I doubt he's as powerful as she wants me to believe.

Miller also owns Gloria's car. I'm certain he paid for all her designer clothes too, and her jewelry. Where does a police chief get that kind of money? Darnell Miller must be bent. I suppose he could have inherited money, but to afford all the luxuries he lavishes on Gloria, the man would've had to come from the Rockefeller lineage. I doubt that. I've come across bent coppers before, and I can sniff them out from a mile away. Miller smells as dirty as a heap of rotting rubbish.

Now that I know who Gloria's lover is, I have no idea what to do next. Confront Gloria? That would be risky. If her lover is corrupt, he won't hesitate to use every method at his disposal to cover up his misdeeds. I'd hoped gaining more information would help somehow. But now I realize that I need to give up on this quest. To keep going might bring trouble, and I can't risk Catriona getting caught in the middle.

So I shut down my computer and crawl into bed with Cat.

I will only use the information I've gathered if Gloria or Darnell Miller forces me to do it. Neither of them can know about my past.

Unless the chief of police has connections I don't know about yet.

Chapter Fourteen

Catriona

On this Monday morning, I'm in the university library scouring books for information that will help me with my dissertation. I've settled on a topic, and soon I will graduate from doctoral student to PhD candidate. That means I need to get a head start on my dissertation. Alex offered to help me, as my unofficial adviser, but he needed to do some paperwork first.

For the past week, Alex has not behaved strangely or gone on secret missions that he calls "work-related research." I let him get away with that because I know he wouldn't keep anything important from me. Whatever he needed to do, it must be exactly what he said.

Hands cover my eyes. "Guess who, darling."

I smile and peel his hands away, then glance up at Alex and pretend to be surprised. "Oh, I thought you were my other boyfriend."

"Hmm. I think I'll take these back." He thrusts a bouquet of daisies in front of me. "Unless you care to apologize."

I grasp the back of his neck and pull his head down so I can press my lips to his. "I'll give you my full apology tonight."

"When we're naked, I hope."

"Aye, of course."

He rests his erse on the table's edge beside me. Glancing around, he sighs with mock disappointment. "I was hoping you'd be in the basement again so we could ruin another flimsy table. But you're on the first floor within sight of the circulation desk."

"And a number of other students."

He picks up my hand, kissing it. "What are the chances I can talk you into doing something very naughty with me?"

"Your chances are excellent—when we're at home."

"What if I can't wait that long?"

I rise and pick up my rucksack. "Let's go home now."

"What about your afternoon classes?"

"*Mhac na galla.* I forgot about that."

Alex's mouth quirks into an amused expression. "I do love it when you curse in Gaelic. Did your brothers teach you to do that?"

"No. My sister Fiona did."

He raises his brows. "The MacTaggart women are a foul-mouthed bunch, eh? I need to meet your family."

Does he want that? I doubt he was being serious, but I wonder if he might actually like to meet my family someday. I've mentioned many of my cousins to him, and he didn't seem shocked by how large the MacTaggart clan is.

I sniff the flowers and smile again. "Thank you for these. They're lovely. But is there a special occasion I forgot about?"

"Do I need a reason to spoil you?"

"Of course not. I love it when you surprise me like this."

He slings an arm around my shoulders as we walk out of the library. "I'll walk you to the humanities building, then run a few errands. I grabbed your list off the refrigerator door this morning."

How many men would volunteer to go grocery shopping? Well, my brothers would. And some of my male cousins too. But I haven't met many other lads who would. Alex is an unusual man, but I love that about him.

We part ways outside the humanities building, and I go to my classes. Both lectures are interesting, but I can't wait for these two hours to be over with so I can go home with Alex. The moment class ends, I snatch up my rucksack and hurry outside to find him, knowing he won't be far away. I see him, but he is not alone. Gloria Harris is talking to him, and while she seems quite pleased with herself, Alex looks the opposite. He isn't angry, not exactly. But he does appear tense and uncomfortable.

"Alex, there you are," I say, trying to sound casual as I approach him. I hook my arm around his and aim a polite smile at Gloria. "How nice to see you again."

The woman smiles in a way that does not seem friendly. "Catriona. Isn't it a coincidence that we all bumped into each other here? I've never been to the campus before."

"Why are you here?" Alex asks. "You still haven't explained that."

Gloria grins, but again, it doesn't seem like a pleasant expression. "I'm here to see you, of course. Have you considered my offer?"

Alex huffs. "Offer? You demanded I shag you."

She laughs. "Honestly, Alex, you're being melodramatic. Yes, I want to have sex with you. But I don't mind at all if you still want to screw Catriona. We could even have a threesome."

"Nothing that you just suggested will ever happen."

"Really?" Gloria moves closer to him. "I have friends in high places, hon. Might not be the smartest idea to tick me off."

"Please. As if I'm frightened of you, the twenty-six-year-old slag who offers herself to any stranger who happens along."

Gloria snaps ramrod straight and puckers her lips. "You'll regret this."

Then she whirls around and stomps away from us.

I look up at Alex. "How did that woman ever find you in the first place? Do you believe the story she told us before about how she accidentally wound up in this town and saw us?"

"Yes, I think I do believe that. Or maybe it's fate punishing me for being a chancer."

"Alex, you are a good man who made mistakes. Donnae take all the blame. Gloria wanted to sleep with you."

"I know. But… Well, let's just forget we ever saw her."

"What if she comes back again?"

He lays a hand over mine on his arm. "Don't worry about Gloria. She likes to stir up trouble, that's all. She will give up once she realizes it's no fun harassing us when we don't give her what she wants."

If Alex believes Gloria will give up soon, then I believe it too.

Once we get home, Alex starts doing things on his laptop computer again, like he's done often lately. I guess his lesson plans have become more of a burden, which makes me wonder if his TA is doing anything at all to help him. Cannae see any other reason why he would need to work so hard every evening.

I go into the bedroom and ring my sister Fiona. We talk for a while and laugh quite a bit because she tells me all the barmy things our siblings and cousins have done lately. Our conversation turns more serious when she tells me that our cousin Logan has been deployed to Iraq in his capacity as a military intelligence officer. That means he might go on dangerous missions, though neither Fiona nor I fully understand what his job entails. I hope he doesn't get deployed for more tours after this, like other people I know back home.

Alex ambles into the bedroom just as I'm saying goodbye to Fiona. I hang up, but I stay in the same position—knees drawn up to my chest, one arm around them.

He sits down beside me on the bed's edge. "What's wrong, love? You look worried."

"I am worried. My cousin Logan, the one who's in the army, has been sent to Iraq."

Alex pulls me against his side and holds me. "I'm sorry, Cat. Can't imagine how stressful that must be, for your cousin or for you. I imagine your whole clan is anxious about it."

"We are. My cousin Magnus is in the army too, but he hasn't been deployed to a war zone yet. That might happen any day, though."

He strokes my hair, which always soothes me. "From the way you described those two blokes, I think they can handle themselves. Try not to worry overmuch."

I wrap my arms around him, snuggling my cheek into the hollow of his shoulder. "As long as I'm with you, I know everything will be all right."

Alex picks me up and cradles me with one arm while he pulls the covers back. Then he lays me down gently and crawls over me to lie down too. I cuddle up to him. He tugs the covers over us both, and soon, I drift off to sleep.

When I wake in the morning, Alex has already made breakfast for us. We don't discuss last night, but instead focus on today and what we plan to do since it's Saturday. Alex wants to go for a drive to explore the areas around Ballesteros that we haven't seen yet. We enjoy our day trip so much that I almost don't want to go home, but I know we have to do that. Though Alex might have a lot of money, I don't want to waste it all today. Could I do that in one day? He never has told me exactly how big his bank account is, only that he's wealthier than most people and that it's family money.

I don't need to know more. Not unless we get married.

But he hasn't asked me that question—or said he loves me.

"What's wrong?" Alex asks. "You look melancholy, which isn't like you. Are you still worried about your cousin?"

"No, it's not that. I just feel… I don't know. That woman Gloria fashes me, that's all."

"Do not let that woman ruin a beautiful day. She won't 'fash' you anymore."

"How can you know that?"

Alex pats my thigh and gives me a reassuring smile. "Because I won't let her harass you anymore. If she tries it, I will report her to the police for stalking."

I don't know if that would work, but Alex is right. I can't let one woman ruin a perfectly beautiful day.

He pats my thigh again. "Feeling better? You're not biting your lip anymore."

"Aye, I feel better. You always know what to say to cheer me up." I lean over to kiss his cheek. "I love you, Alex."

"Yes, I know."

That's all he says. What else can I do? I've never been good at making anyone confide in me, and I donnae like to force the issue. But the longer he avoids telling me how he feels, the more I realize I shouldn't let him sidestep his feelings. But for today, I will enjoy the time I have with him. Tomorrow…

He'd better start talking.

Chapter Fifteen

Alex

Catriona wants me to say I love her. Even I am not blind and deaf enough to have missed the signs. Back when she'd told me she's in love with me, I could dismiss that as… ah… nothing I need to worry about. I know I'm a bloody stupid arse and a bastard. Cat should have left me ages ago. Instead, she stayed and loved me and forgave me for not sharing my past with her. And now she has said those four words.

I love you, Alex.

So what if she said that? I didn't ask her to do it, which means I don't need to say it in return. Or maybe it means I should have said it yesterday when she spoke the words. It's too late now. Maybe I might possibly have wanted to… I don't know what I wanted.

Today, the morning after Catriona dropped her word bomb on me, she has gone to the campus to do more research in the library. That leaves me with nothing to do since this is Sunday. I have no classes to teach and no lesson plans to, ah, plan. I sit in our living room, watching ruddy awful television shows. And all the while, I keep slipping my hand into my trouser pocket to finger the diamond ring I'd meant to give to Cat on that cursed night. Do I still want to give it to her? What if I do? Maybe I don't. The fact that I carry it around in my pocket every day could mean nothing.

Have I lost my mind? I should probably have myself committed.

The doorbell rings while I'm still obsessing over what I should or should not have told Catriona and when or when not I should have done that. I mute the telly and shuffle to the door, swinging it open.

And I freeze.

The bloke staring back at me… I recognize him. I took photographs of this man and Gloria Harris going at it like chimpanzees on acid. Yes, the chief of police stands on my doorstep, glowering at me.

"Yes?" I say, as if I don't give a toss. "If you're selling band candy, I've already bought several cartons of that."

"Band candy?" Darnell Miller shakes his head. "Do I look like a high school nerd?"

"No, but you do seem like the sort who would play the oboe."

"Don't get cute with me, dirtbag."

"Why not? I am very cute, according to women." I casually slide my hands into my trouser pockets. "Just ask Gloria Harris."

"That's why I'm here. You upset her, and I'm gonna make it right."

"Are you?" I lean against the doorjamb, affecting an air of disinterest. "Go on, make it right."

Miller lifts his chin and smiles with smug self-assurance. "You think you're so damn smart, don't you? Well, I know who you really are."

"How nice for you."

"Cut the crap." Miller jabs a finger into my chest. "When Gloria told me what you did to her, I contacted my buddy at the Metropolitan Police in London."

"Interesting. You're quite an enterprising chap, aren't you?"

He stabs that finger into my chest again. "You won't be so full of piss and vinegar after you hear what I found out."

"I don't think you understand the phrase. Piss and vinegar means I have energy and enthusiasm." I give him my best sarcastic smile. "Thank you for the compliment, Chief Miller."

"Stop trying to distract me. You're an arrogant jackass, and I'm going to take you down so many pegs that you won't know what hit you."

This man is a moron. But sometimes that sort can become the most dangerous enemies. They take irrational risks because they are imbeciles.

"Tell me what you want," I say. "This conversation is growing tiresome."

"Fine by me." He reaches inside his jacket and pulls out a sheaf of rolled-up papers. Then he thrusts them at me. "Look at this."

Naturally, he sounds pleased with himself. Very pleased.

I pluck the papers from his hand, unrolling the pages. Then I stare at the words printed on the top sheet. Stare at them for so long that my eyes begin to burn because I've stopped blinking. How in the world? He can't—This is not possible, yet the evidence stares right back at me from the page I'm holding. But I will not give this cretin the pleasure of making me angry. That's what he wants, I'm sure. Probably so he can arrest me for assaulting a police officer.

I roll up the papers and offer them to him. "That's an interesting story, but I prefer fiction."

Miller sneers at me. "I've got you dead to rights, and we both know it."

"Things that happened in another lifetime have no bearing on the present. Why don't you distract yourself by fucking Gloria?" I feign surprise. "Oh, that's right. She prefers me. Bad luck, mate."

His face turns crimson, and he snarls words through his clenched teeth. "Wait'll I show this to your cute little girlfriend."

"Go on, show it to her." I slap his arm. "She loves a good comedy."

"Maybe I can do better than showing her your record." He twists his mouth into a nasty expression. "I'll make sure she has a record too."

"Oh, yes, I'm so bloody terrified."

I managed to speak those words in my best sarcastic tone, but I wonder. Can he do what he suggested? He is the chief of police, and I'm not at all sure that I can leverage those photos to get him off my back. I need more than pictures of him shagging Gloria. Am I prepared to become a blackmailer? For Catriona, I will do anything. This cretin doesn't understand what I've been through, the things I've done, or how far I'll go to protect the people who matter to me.

"Good night, Chief Miller," I say as I step back and start to close the door.

"Wait up, wiseass. Do you want your girlfriend to go to prison?"

I stop with the door halfway closed. "What are you talking about?"

"Here's the deal." He pushes past me to enter the house, and I'm too stunned to stop him. Miller slams the door shut. "If you don't do what I say, I'll invent some charges for your girl. She'll spend a good long while in the pokey. That means prison. Hard time."

I seize his shirt collar and smack him into the wall. "Careful, Chief. I'm not a mild-mannered professor who will crumble under pressure. If you try to take me down, I will make sure you go with me."

And if he hurts Catriona, even makes her shed one tear, I will snap his fucking neck.

"What I want shouldn't be hard for you to do," he says. "Nothing you haven't done before. Just get something for me."

"Such as?"

He digs a folded-up sheet of paper out of his trouser pocket and raises it for me to see. "Get me this, and I'll forget about your girl and your record. You have twenty-four hours."

Miller tucks the folded paper into the breast pocket of my shirt.

I back away from him and watch as the wanker saunters out of the house. Maybe I should've stopped the blighter and beaten him until blood covered his face. But violence has never been my strong suit, and assaulting Miller won't solve my problem. It would give him cause to arrest me and probably Cat too.

She won't be home for a while yet, which gives me time to search for a solution. I grab my handheld video camera and get in my car to follow Darnell Miller. I would've thought a police chief would spot me tailing him, but Miller spends the entire drive back to his house talking on his mobile—angrily, based on his gesticulating hands and the way he shakes his head. He swerves into the other lane three times. Luckily, there are no other cars near enough for him to cause an accident.

Police are meant to care about public safety. But no, I am not surprised that Miller only cares about himself.

Though I'm not adept at tailing someone, I've watched enough television shows to understand the basics. Picking someone's pocket? I could do that blindfolded. But surveillance is outside of my wheelhouse. I slow down as Miller turns onto a quiet street on the outskirts of town, on the opposite side of Ballesteros from where Gloria lives. He must be going home. I've slowed down enough that I'm still two blocks away when Miller pulls into the driveway of a small house. I turn down a side street and park along the curb, then walk to the house I assume Miller owns. His car still sits in the driveway, but I don't see the man himself. He must have gone inside already.

I head down another side street and find that I can access his unfenced backyard quite easily. Employing my less than prodigious surveillance skills, I creep up to the house and peek into the windows as I make my way toward the front. I've just reached the kitchen when Miller stomps into that room, snarling at whoever he's talking to on his mobile. Miller moves closer, and I can finally hear what he says.

"Gimme a break, Gloria." He grasps the nape of his neck. "I'm trying to get it for you. Maybe if you hadn't bled me dry buying that house and your goddamn car, I'd be able to give you what you want."

Miller snaps his flip phone shut, scowling at the floor, and shoves the mobile into his pocket.

Gloria bled him dry? I wonder if she's the one demanding that he steal a diamond necklace for her.

The police chief shoves both hands into his hair, his shoulders sagging. Then he brings out his mobile and makes a call. "Hey, baby, it's me. Need to see you now, please." His frown mutates into a sly smile. "Oh, yeah, you know exactly what I need. Let me tell you all the things I'll do to you."

I try not to listen while he describes in graphic detail what he wants to do with whatever woman is on the other end of that call. Did Gloria ring him to apologize?

Miller chuckles. "Don't worry about Gloria. She's a conniving little snake, but I'll be free of her soon. Then we can go away together like we planned because I'll sell that damn house and the car to finance our getaway." He listens, and his smile broadens into a grin. "Oh, yeah. My money and yours, that's all we need."

He disconnects the call and sets about gathering food items—champagne, strawberries, chocolates, whipped cream, and other sensual delicacies. He means to seduce the woman he was talking to on the phone. It's not Gloria, which means this man has two mistresses. *Blimey.* Where does he find the energy to please two women?

When Miller leaves the kitchen, carrying his romantic supplies, I sneak around to the living room windows. The police chief walks into that room a moment later. He turns on a stereo system, and music full of bass beats and lingering saxophone notes emanates from it. Sounds like a sodding porno film in there. Miller sets up his mini buffet of treats and puts the champagne inside a bucket of ice. Then he sits down on a recliner and shuts his eyes.

And I wait. Five minutes. Ten minutes. I lean against the house and slump onto the grass. Fifteen minutes. Twenty minutes. Just as I'm about to give up and go home, a car pulls into the driveway. From my position at the corner of the house, I can see into the living room and the porch.

A beautiful redhead emerges from the luxury vehicle and sashays up to the door, ringing the bell.

I hop up just in time to see Miller race out of the living room, heading toward the front door. The second he pulls it open, the woman flies into his arms and kisses him. Miller picks her up and carries her into the living room while they keep kissing with so much passion that I wonder if they can still breathe.

Grabbing my video camera, I start recording. Maybe what I film will never be useful, but I need to do something.

The lovers begin to remove their clothes, though they pause now and then to shove food into each other's mouths. Once they're naked, Miller pops the champagne cork and hands the bottle to his lover. He lies down on the sofa. The redhead straddles him and pours the bubbly onto his chest, then licks it off.

I think I'm going to be sick.

But I keep recording as she mounts his cock and the fucking begins in earnest.

While I watch—strictly to make sure I keep them in the frame—I realize I've seen this woman before. I'd met her briefly a few weeks before my first day at Ballesteros, at the mixer for new professors, which was hosted by the university trustees. I'd seen her again a few months ago at a fundraiser for the humanities department.

That woman is married to one of the trustees.

Oh, this is perfect. I have proof that the chief of police is shagging a trustee's wife. All I need to do is send a copy of this video to her husband. I've met the man, and he is a toerag, definitely the jealous type.

I've recorded enough of Miller and his lover's antics. To spare myself from vomiting on the hydrangea bush beside me, I turn off my video camera and hurry back to my car. Cat will be home soon, so I drive a bit faster than I should to make sure I arrive before she does.

Maybe I have a chance to save us both after all.

Chapter Sixteen

Catriona

I come home to find Alex busily cooking dinner. He seems more relaxed than I've seen him in quite a while, and he even hums while he works. As much as I love his new attitude, I can't help wondering what inspired it. Alex can be hard to pin down. Even after almost two years of living with him, I often feel like I'll never fully understand him.

"Welcome home," he says with a grin. "Dinner will be served in ten minutes."

I set down my rucksack and kick off my shoes. "Whatever you're cooking smells wonderful. What are we celebrating?"

"Nothing. Do I need a reason to treat you to a homemade meal?"

"We eat at home most of the time, but you don't go all out for an average dinner."

"I love to spoil you, darling. You know that."

Aye, Alex does enjoy doing that. I love letting him do it.

We share a wonderful meal, then relax on the sofa to watch television for a while. "Just until our food settles," he says. I know we will make love tonight. I can see that twinkle in his eyes, the one that means he wants a feast of sex too. We haven't had a poke in almost a week, and I've wondered why. The answer doesn't matter anymore. Alex is here with me, and he's his old self again. That's all I need to know.

Alex shuts off the television and leads me into the bedroom, then strips the covers off the bed. He sits down at the foot and leans back to rest his elbows on the mattress. "Strip for me, love. Please. Go slowly so I can relish every moment."

I unzip my jeans and push them down over my hips, taking my time and letting them fall to my ankles. Then I kick them away and unhook the buttons on my blouse one by one.

Alex is breathing harder now, and I can see the bulge growing inside his trousers.

Freeing the last button, I slide my hand inside my blouse and slowly push it off one shoulder, then the other. The shirt flutters to the floor.

"You are so beautiful," he says, his voice a husky murmur. "I love your body, Cat. It's a work of art."

I remove my socks next. While I reach behind me to unhook my bra, Alex licks his lips and tracks every movement I make. Since he wanted me to take my time, I release every tiny clasp slowly, pausing between each one and rolling my hips too because I love the way his gaze is glued to my body. By the time I slide the bra off my shoulders and toss it away, Alex is rubbing his cock through his jeans.

The hunger on his face makes my sex throb.

I slide a finger inside the waistband of my knickers.

Alex leaps off the bed and rushes toward me, yanking my knickers off with a single rough jerk of his fingers. The fabric rips apart. He snatches the ruined underwear off my body and flings it aside. Then he sweeps me up in his arms and drops me onto the bed.

While I bounce, laughter bubbles out of me. "I love it when ye get so randy ye cannae wait another second."

He tears off his clothes faster than I've ever seen him do that before. "Your striptease drove me mad. You are the sexiest woman on the face of the earth."

I glance at his erection and cannae help licking my lips. "I want to taste you tonight, Alex."

"All right. But don't make me come."

"I won't. Need you inside me right after this."

I rise to my knees and wave a hand in a come-hither gesture. He approaches the bed, halting right in front of me. I waddle closer, then rest my erse on the mattress with my legs hanging over the edge. His cock hovers right in front of my face, its sleek length curving upward slightly and the glistening tip now a rosy red. I clasp the base of his erection and slide my lips over his crown, taking him all the way into my mouth. The flavor and feel of his skin on my tongue makes me moan. I place my free hand on his inner thigh and begin massaging my way up toward his *bagais* until I can palm his sac.

Alex groans deeply.

Giving his sac a swift tug, I shift my hand down to his thigh and resume massaging his flesh. All the while, I lick and suck his hard length, devouring him while soft grunting noises emerge from my throat. Cannae help it. I always love tasting Alex and driving him barmy with the need to come. When I glance up at him, he has his eyes half-closed and wears an expression of pure pleasure.

I pull my mouth away from his *slat*. "Mm, Alex, I could you feast on you for hours. You taste so good, and you have the most beautiful cock in the world."

"You're full of rubbish," he says, his voice strained. "But I like it."

Taking him into my mouth again, I begin pumping his length with one hand while I work him with my mouth too. I watch his expression as it morphs from sheer pleasure to a sort of pain that I know means he will come soon.

So I release him and crawl backward on the bed. "Time to shag, Alex."

"Oh, yes, it is time."

Alex grabs a condom from the nightstand drawer, rolling it on quickly. Then he kneels between my legs and runs his hands up and down them, his touch so delicate that a warm tingle sweeps over me from head to toe. He slides his hands under my knees and lifts until I bend them, planting my heels on the bed. When he urges me to spread my thighs for him, I do it without hesitation. As he lowers onto his hands and knees, his cock grazes my cleft, and I instinctively arch my back. That warm tingle spreads into my folds and deeper to penetrate my sex, while Alex bends his head to kiss me tenderly.

"I'd love to taste you," he murmurs, "but I might come too soon if I do that. The way you look and sound when you climax drives me mad."

"Just take me, Alex." I clench the sheets in my fingers. "Now. Please."

He pushes inside me with such delicacy that my heart pounds, and I fist my hands even harder until my fingers start to ache, but I donnae care. His length fills me up, and when he lays his body on top of mine, his chest rubs on my hard nipples.

"Oh, Alex," I moan. "You feel so good inside me."

"I love the feel of your body wrapped around me." He begins a measured pace of thrusting while he frames my head with his hands, and our gazes align as if an invisible thread binds us. "Catriona, my darling, my love."

My heart skips a beat. Did he say… I cannae think about that anymore because he's kissing me now, delicately, sweetly, while he keeps thrusting and the sensation of his hardness inside me steals every other thought I might've had. I grip his biceps as his tongue coils around mine in a slow and sensual dance, teasing me and loving me at the same time.

The climax sweeps through me in slow motion, my inner muscles gripping him in softly rolling waves as a gasping cry tumbles from my lips. Alex rises onto his straight arms and thrusts harder and faster until he comes with a strangled shout. Our lovemaking might not have been earth-shattering, but it was more intimate than anything we've shared before.

Alex collapses onto me, his head nestled against my throat and his cock still inside me.

I comb my fingers through his hair. "Alex, I love you so much."

"Cat, I—"

The phone rings.

He pulls away from me and snatches the handset off the nightstand. "Hello?"

While he listens to the caller, his expression shifts from relaxed to almost stony, as if he doesn't like whatever the caller has told him. He hangs up without saying goodbye.

I push up onto my elbows. "What was that about?"

"Nothing, love." He gets rid of the condom and kneels between my thighs again. "It's time for me to feast on you, darling. Your sweet cream is the most delicious dessert any man could enjoy."

"But Alex—"

He shoves his face between my thighs and latches on to my nub, then begins suckling it while he teases my folds with his fingers. I meant to ask him something, but suddenly, I cannae remember what it was. He drives me toward the heights of ecstasy again so swiftly that the power of it robs me of breath and scatters my wits. I come harder this time, my body bowing inward while my feet lift off the mattress and cries erupt out of me. He keeps tormenting my clit until my voice goes hoarse and I'm sobbing from the intensity of what he's done to me.

Alex lies down beside me, facing me, and tugs my body against him. "I'll give you a few minutes to recover before I do that again. And after the second time, I'll have recovered enough to sink my cock into your sweet flesh again."

"We've never done it more than twice."

"Tonight is special." He circles his finger around my nipple, his touch so delicate that it makes my heart thud. "I mean to show you everything I can't say."

"Donnae understand."

"Hush, love. Let me demonstrate for you."

I don't get the chance to say anything else. Whenever Alex touches me, I lose my mind. But when he makes love to me the way he's done tonight, I know he must feel what I do. He must love me as much as I love him. Why he can't say it, I don't know. But for this one night, I will let him show me however he wants and I won't question him.

Not tonight. But soon, he will tell me. I'll make sure of it.

Alex makes love to me for hours, with breaks to eat savory snacks and drink Talisker from the bottle. I've never been with any other man who would treat me the way Alex does, as if I'm the only woman in the world who matters, as if he never wants to be with anyone else. He whispers the sweetest words to me throughout our marathon in bed, and I've never felt closer to him than I do now.

We fall asleep tangled up in each other, and in the sheets. I sink into a deep slumber spiced up by sensual dreams of Alex. I wake in the morning feeling so good that I think I must still be asleep. But I'm not. Alex gave me this feeling. Now he lies beside me with one arm draped over my hip. Since I'm facing him, I decide to just lie here watching him sleep, loving his relaxed and almost innocent expression, as if all the things he's been afraid to tell me no longer fash him.

I could watch him sleep for hours. The masculine beauty of his body takes my breath away, and so does the idea of rousing him so we can have another poke before breakfast. But instead of doing that, I leave him sleeping and slip into a dressing gown. Then I slink out of the bedroom to make breakfast for us. Alex often rises first, which means he usually cooks for us both. Today, I want to surprise him with a good meal full of protein that will give us both plenty of energy for the day ahead. We expended a lot of calories last night.

On my way to the kitchen, I take a moment to gaze out the picture windows and appreciate the view. Everything seems more beautiful and more meaningful today. I know Alex loves me, even though he has never spoken the words, because he proved that to me last night with his expressions and his body. As I trot into the kitchen, I already have a menu in mind for our post-sex meal.

Will Alex propose to me someday? I have an intuition that he will. Maybe I'll become Catriona Thorne soon. Of course, he'll need to meet my family first. I know they will love him almost as much as I do.

As I whip up our breakfast, I can't help dancing and humming along to the songs on the radio. Since I know how to cook these dishes from memory, I allow myself to fantasize about what our wedding might be like, how handsome Alex will look in a tuxedo, and how happy we will be.

Someone knocks on the front door so loudly that it rattles.

I race to the door and swing it open. All the blood in body seems to have turned to ice, and I stare numbly at the two men standing before me.

The police officers stare at me with stony expressions. One of them speaks. "Catriona MacTaggart?"

"Aye, that's me."

He brings out a pair of handcuffs. "You're under arrest for suspicion of smuggling antiquities."

Chapter Seventeen

Alex

I'd been lying in bed, enjoying the aromas of whatever food Cat had prepared for breakfast, when I heard someone banging on the front door. I pulled on my jeans and a T-shirt, then ran into the living room, meaning to reach the door before Cat. But she got there first. Two police officers stood just outside the threshold, each wearing a stern expression and carrying a firearm strapped to his hip.

"You've got it wrong," I say as I come up beside Catriona. "You don't want to arrest her."

"Stay out of this, Dr. Thorne. We have our orders."

He knows my name, which might give Catriona the idea that I know this wanker. I've never seen him before. But I do know his boss, Chief of Police Darnell Miller, and I have no doubts he sent these men. Whether they realize the charges are trumped up, I have no idea. Would they care if they did know? My only concern right now is to stop them from taking Cat.

I squint at the bloke who had spoken and repeat the words I'd said a moment ago, this time with more menace in my voice. "You've got it wrong."

The officers eye me with their lantern jaws tightly set and their gazes narrowed on me. Do they really think that will intimidate me? They're fools if they do.

"She's coming with us," the officer who'd spoken a moment ago says. "You can visit her in county lockup."

"At least let her get dressed," I snarl.

"Can't. Got orders." The other officer, the one who had hand-cuffed Cat, spears me with a knife-sharp glare that does not frighten me. "Orders from the top."

"You are making a mistake that you will regret."

"Doubt it, pal. You're not as smart as you think."

The officers drag her out of the apartment, despite the fact she's wearing only a dressing gown and not even a pair of slippers. Though I want to beat those men senseless for treating her like a criminal, I know that will do no good. If I'm arrested, I can't fight to get her released. We don't need lawyers. All I need is the video I recorded yesterday.

I want to follow those bastards to the jail, but I know that's the wrong thing to do right now. Instead, I finish getting dressed and grab the videotape, then climb into my car and drive too fast and too recklessly on my way to the home of Darnell Miller. I have a hunch he will be there. The man is not a hard-working professional, but a chancer who will do anything to get what he wants. That suggests to me that he will still be at home. I would bet all the money I have that he never shows up to work before ten o'clock.

And it's barely seven right now.

Since I no longer need to be stealthy, I slam my foot down on the brake pedal, screeching to a halt along the curb in front of Miller's house. I don't give a fuck that everyone in the vicinity might have heard that noise. By the time I stomp up the steps onto the porch, Miller has swung his front door open.

When he sees me, he scuffles backward and tries to close the door in my face.

I kick it open before the latch clicks into place and stalk into the house. Miller keeps backing up, apparently aiming for the living room behind him. Kicking the door shut, I seize Miller's shirt and drag him closer.

Spittle sprays from my lips as I snarl, "Call off your dogs. Do it right now. Release Catriona immediately, or I will make sure Raymond Anderson knows you've been fucking his wife, thanks to the video I took of you two going at it. I doubt Connie will want to shag you ever again once her husband knows about the two of you."

"You don't know the Andersons. You're lying."

"Am I? Raymond Anderson is a trustee of Ballesteros University, where I work. I've met him and his wife more than once." I shake Miller hard. "You have no idea who you're dealing with. You claim to know who I am and what I've done, but that is clearly a lie. If you knew the whole truth, you wouldn't have tried this blackmail scheme."

Miller's face has turned a few shades paler. His expression has gone slack too, a clear indication that he thought I'd be an easy mark for his blackmail-slash-burglary scheme.

"Release Catriona," I hiss. "And make certain there are no blemishes on her record. If I find out you've so much as mentioned her name in any reports, I will hunt you down and punish you."

"Okay, okay," Miller says, holding his hands up in surrender. "Relax, she won't have any record. Forget about that diamond necklace. Gloria said she'd tell Connie Anderson I was sleeping with her too. She knows I swore to Connie she was the only one."

"I don't give a toss about your infidelity problems."

"What I'm saying is please don't send the video to Raymond. He'll murder me—professionally, at least."

A harsh laugh bursts out of me. "Am I meant to feel sorry for you? I hope Anderson ruins your life." I let go of Miller and move toward the door. "Do what you promised. I think even your minuscule brain can comprehend the consequences if you renege."

"Yeah, I get it. Your girl will be released within the hour." When I keep glaring flaming daggers at him, he picks up the phone and dials. "Ronnie? Yeah, let the girl go, free and clear."

I walk out the door and slam it shut behind me.

By the time I arrive at the county jail, most of my fury has settled down to a low simmer. Every time I think of Darnell Miller, though, I wind up strangling the steering wheel and gritting my teeth. He deserves to be arrested and charged with some sort of crime, any sort, just to make sure he can't do this to anyone else. But I can't go to any type of authority to report him.

I had made one stop on my way to the county jail. Raymond Anderson lives in a mansion on the wealthiest street in town, which only has half a dozen homes. I have no trouble finding the right one. Parking on an adjacent street, I jog to Anderson's home and set my package on the doorstep, then ring the bell. I return to my car and drive past the Anderson home just in time to see the man himself pick up the package. Since I had included a note that said "Darnell Miller is not your friend and your wife knows why," I feel confident Anderson will watch the video.

I race to the county jail, which seems to be run by the sheriff's department, and I see blokes wearing those uniforms when I walk inside the building. But I also meet one of the toerags who had dragged Cat away.

He smirks at me. "I'll go get your girl. Maybe she won't be your girl anymore, though, huh? Probably realizes what a prick you are now that she got thrown in the clink."

Though I want to snarl at him, and possibly throttle the knob, I maintain a neutral expression and relaxed demeanor. And I wait. Minutes tick by on the clock on the wall. What is taking so bloody long? My neutral expression might be transforming into a stony look, but I can't help that. I refuse to let anyone see my anger.

The officer and Catriona emerge from the cell block or whatever they call it. The officer says, "Here she is."

My fingers curl into my palms, then tighten into fists. Cat looks bedraggled and frightened, still wearing nothing but her dressing gown.

The officer gives her a shove, pushing her toward me while he looks at her. "Alex Thorne is seriously bad news. You'd be better off running as fast as you can from him, before he drags you down into the quicksand, for good next time."

"Shut up," I hiss as I throw an arm around Cat's shoulders and guide her toward the exit. Darnell Miller must have shared what he knows about my past with this twat and probably his twat partner too. "You'll regret this, the lot of you."

Yes, I will find a way to make sure Miller's henchmen suffer too.

At the car, I stop to ensure Cat's dressing gown is securely tied, then whisk my hands up and down her arms. "Christ, you're barely dressed. You must be freezing."

I wrap my arms around her, and for a moment, I just hold her. What might've happened… It doesn't matter. It's over now. I kiss her forehead and help her into the car, then snatch a fleece throw from the backseat and drape it over her. Then I drive us home. I don't speak, and neither does Cat. But I know my reckoning has arrived.

Once we get home, I order her to have a shower and get dressed. While she does that, I slump onto an armchair, lodge my elbows on my thighs, and stare down at the floor. Though I hear Cat's footsteps as she enters the living room and the slight thump as she drops onto the sofa, it takes me a moment before I can raise my head to look at her.

"Bloody hell, Cat." I knife my hands through my hair and hurl myself backward against the chair. "I'm sorry. This is all my fault."

"How?"

I'm still gazing at her, but my voice refuses to work. She looks so young and innocent and sad, not to mention thoroughly confused. I want to hold her, swear to her everything is fine, but that would be a lie. Staying with me will destroy her.

The words I want to say get stuck in my throat. *I love you, Cat, please marry me.* She shouldn't do that. I can't let her do it, and I can't let her go on loving me.

"How is it your fault?" she asks.

"It's complicated," I say carefully. "The details aren't important right now. Just know that you are not going to jail. I will not allow that to happen. And your arrest record will be expunged."

She goes perfectly still, her unblinking gaze nailed to mine. "You know why I was arrested."

"It doesn't matter now." I rise and shut my eyes, frozen in place while I struggle to figure out what to tell her. Not the truth. Which leaves me with one agonizing choice. I marshal all my willpower to do what must be done. Then I kneel in front of her and meet her gaze. "I'm not going to explain any of this. You'll either trust me to take care of things, or you won't."

Is that my voice? I sound so cool and unaffected, but I suppose that's how I need to be right now.

"That's not good enough, Alex. I deserve the truth. I demand it."

"I can't do that, Catriona."

"Yes, you can." She slants toward me until our noses almost touch and aims her fiery gaze straight into mine. "Either tell me what is going on, or I will walk out that door and never come back."

Coldness floods through me, chilling me down to the core of my soul. If I even have one of those. "Do what you need to do."

"Dammit, Alex." She slaps her hands on my chest and pushes with all her strength, but she can't move me. "Why won't you talk to me? All I want is the truth."

"And that's the one thing I can't give you. Not today. Maybe never."

Cat gawps at me, searching my gaze for something that she clearly can't find. That would be my nonexistent soul, I imagine. I see it in her eyes the second she makes her decision. "Then there's only one thing left to say. Goodbye, Alex."

A pang stabs into my chest, as sharp and cold as a knife's blade. But I rise and take a step backward, giving a bang-on impression of a heartless bastard. I don't even move when she pushes past me to go into the bedroom and gather her possessions. I stand here frozen in place, feeling numb and yet relieved at the same time. I'd always known I couldn't have her forever.

Catriona hauls a suitcase to the doorway and rests her hand on the knob, glancing back at me. "I'll come back for the rest of my things while you're at work. This is the last time you'll see me, Alex."

I swear she's pleading with me to beg her to stay, in her eyes if not her expression. But I'm an arrogant arsehole, so she probably isn't doing that. "Goodbye, Catriona."

She walks out the door.

For several minutes, I don't move, rooted to the spot where I'd stood when Catriona MacTaggart severed our relationship. I made her do it. I needed her to do it. Maybe I had the strength to stand up to Darnell Miller, but when it comes to the woman I love, I am a coward through and through. So yes, I make sure to be elsewhere when Cat returns for the rest of her belongings.

No, I can't watch her leave me.

I do tail Catriona to the airport, though, and watch as she shuffles into the terminal. Then I wait in the car park so I can watch her plane take off, ferrying her back to Scotland. Maybe I should be happy. I got what I wanted. The only woman I will ever love has left me, and I can go back to being a loner with a dodgy background.

But I can't go back. My life will never be the same again.

Chapter Eighteen

Catriona

My family meets me at the Inverness airport. I'd rung my sister Fiona to tell her I was coming home, and I couldn't stop myself from crying while I talked to her. So naturally, she told everyone, and I wind up being greeted by not just my five siblings and my parents, but also a number of my cousins and aunts and uncles. Even my grandparents show up.

By the time the plane landed, I'd recovered my composure. No, I will not let Alex Thorne ruin my life. I love him, but I will get over that one day soon. Aye, my heart will ache for him, but not forever. I mean to move on.

How long will that take?

My family waits for me just outside the terminal doors, and the second I step out there, my mother drags me into a suffocating hug. She kisses my cheek and babbles things I can't understand. Though I receive similar treatment from my sisters, I don't expect that from my brothers. But they each hug me fiercely and vow to "skelp" the "*bod ceann*" who hurt me. I'd rather beat Alex with my own fists because the dickhead deserves it, but I appreciate the sentiment from my brothers.

I love Alex Thorne. Only time will ease the pain.

For the next week, I mostly hide in my bedroom, in the house where I'd grown up, and try to forget about that man. Aye, the betrayal is still too fresh for me to move past it yet. So I lie in bed, hugging the bears Alex had given me, and I cry.

On the seventh day of my self-imposed isolation, I force myself to go out into the world. I start by having breakfast with my family instead of sneaking into the kitchen to steal a snack. Then I accept Fiona and Jamie's invitation to go for a walk and get some fresh air. My sisters use that time to blether about our clan's antics, and aye, hearing all the good gossip does cheer me up a wee bit. My brothers do their part too—by recommending lads I might want to date. I'm not ready for that. I slept with the same man for the better part of two years, and I cannae sweep that all aside, not just yet. But I love them all the more for trying.

Though I've stopped hiding in my room, I still hug those bears every night while I fall asleep.

After a month of missing that man and sometimes crying over the loss, I decide enough is enough. Why should I let Alex Thorne make the rest of my life miserable? I'm young and bonnie and clever, three things any worthwhile man should appreciate. Since I'll be leaving for Edinburgh soon, to continue my doctoral studies, I'll have a much larger pool of lads to choose from which means I will definitely forget about *that* man. I still haven't told anyone the name of the *bod ceann* who broke my heart. But I need to call him something since everyone keeps mentioning him, and their nicknames for him are ridiculous. Lachlan calls him "the wee shit I'm going to batter one day." If I invent my own nickname for Alex, maybe everyone will stop talking about him.

Three weeks before I'm meant to leave for Edinburgh, I announce my new name for Alex. My family is having a barbecue, and my youngest sister, Jamie, gives me an opening.

"When will ye ever tell us that British scunner's name?" she asks. "We have a right to know."

"No, you don't," I say. "The British Bastard doesnae deserve to have his name spoken."

I think my relatives have decided the Limey Louse drove me off my head, and they mean to humor me whenever I mention him. Aye, I just created another nickname for him. A few days later, I invent yet another one when my cousin Iain asks how I'm recovering from my heartbreak. I tell him, "The Soulless Sassenach will never fash me again. I'm getting on with my life."

The move to Edinburgh is temporary, only until I finish my dissertation and earn my PhD. Then I will find a job as an archaeologist, either in the field or as a teacher, and my life will go on in spite of what the British Bastard did to me. During my first week on campus, I meet my two supervisors who will guide me through the rest of my program. Luckily, they've arranged it so I won't need to start over and all the work I'd done in America will count toward my doctorate. That means the Soulless Sassenach has not destroyed my professional dreams, even if he did shatter my heart.

But no, I don't cry anymore when I think of him. Anger has replaced the heartbreak.

That's why I decide to exorcise the demon once and for all. My sisters reluctantly help me gather what I need, and they watch me perform the ritual. I've acquired a small pile of twigs and a bottle of kerosene. Now I light the twigs with the flammable liquid, and once the flames have grown to a good height, I bring out the teddy bears Alex had given me. Then I douse them with kerosene and drop them onto the fire.

Yes, Alex no longer exists in my world.

As the months go by, I do date, though not often. That has nothing to do with the Limey Louse. I'm so busy with my dissertation and field work that I have little time leftover for personal matters. Who needs romance? It's a waste of time. I want to spend my life researching and preserving the past as well as teaching others about the rich and exciting history of our country. That's all the satisfaction I need. The fact that I occasionally dream of Alex, and those dreams are intensely erotic, does not mean I pine for him. The lads I date might not be as good in bed, but at least they don't hide their pasts from me or get me arrested.

Never will I tell anyone that every night as I'm falling asleep, I pray I'll dream of Alex Thorne, or that when I'm alone in my room, I often push myself to orgasm while fantasizing about him. Fantasies donnae mean I still have feelings for him. I absolutely do not.

But sometimes I remember our last night together, and I wonder. When he had whispered "Catriona, my darling, my love," it hadn't felt like an offhanded statement. I believed he had meant that he loved me, though he couldn't say it outright. Whatever Alex felt or almost said doesn't matter anymore.

The British Bastard will never again darken my doorstep.

Chapter Nineteen

Alex

What did I do when Catriona MacTaggart left me? I erased her from my mind and went back to the way I'd been before the lass with the fire in her eyes and in her soul wrecked my perfectly arranged life. I've got it all rearranged, back to the way I want it. So what if I didn't leave my loft for three days after that and rang the dean to tell him I have the flu and I can't teach my classes or deal with office hours for the rest of the week? I do feel a touch feverish. The sodding thermometer is wrong.

I love Cat, but I let her believe the opposite. Now I need to deal with the consequences of my actions. Maybe I should have explained everything to her, even my past, and let her decide whether she wanted to stay with me. No, that would've exacerbated the disaster I had already caused. Do I actually love her? Not sure I'm capable of that depth of feeling, so I probably imagined I felt that way because she insisted on telling me she loved me. Yes, that's what happened.

While I pretend—ah, recuperate from the flu, I receive good news. The local newspaper announces that the chief of police has tendered his resignation and has not announced yet where he will go next. To the nick, I hope. But I rather doubt the blighter will ever be arrested for his crimes. At the very least, I hope Raymond Anderson has gotten that wanker blacklisted so he can never work in law enforcement again. As for Miller's henchmen, I might have sort of planted a few incriminating items in their lockers at the police station, items that might have led to the new interim chief terminating their employment. I doubt either of them will get another job in law enforcement.

So what if that was a dirty trick? Those toerags conspired with their boss to frame an innocent woman for antiquities smuggling. They deserve to suffer for that. A darker and much less forgiving part of me wishes I'd strangled the lot of them. Whatever faults I might have, which are admittedly many and varied, I am not a killer.

A con artist, yes. But not a murderer. Well, former con artist. My days of picking pockets and swindling wealthy individuals have been over for a long time.

The week after Cat—ah, a certain person left the country, I realize I need a change of location too. I will never go back to the UK. I'm not wanted by the Met, never even served time, but I don't feel comfortable returning to the scene of my past crimes. I could go to Canada, or even Europe, but that doesn't appeal to me either. I quit my job at Ballesteros University and seek a new position at a different American institution. It's a college that doesn't even offer graduate programs, but I don't give a toss about that. Living in a small town where no one knows me seems like the safest course right now.

How do I spend the years after I lost the love of my life? By becoming the bastard Catriona thinks I am. I pawn the engagement ring and ignore the pang in my chest when I do that. Then I proceed to cultivate a persona that seems most likely to protect me from ever suffering that sort of pain ever again. I adopt an attitude of breezy sarcasm, as if I don't give a fuck about anything or anyone other than myself. Oddly, college girls love that. The silly birds try to seduce me by batting their lashes and speaking in a huskier tone while they ask if I want to "get busy" or "hook up." I decline their advances in my breezily sarcastic way. And those moronic females adore me even more after I rebuff them. Women are insane, and I will never date any of them ever again. I certainly will not marry one.

But I do occasionally find an anonymous partner for a few hours. We always go to a hotel far from where I live. Whether or not I enjoy those encounters is irrelevant. Perhaps I occasionally consider the possibility that I'm punishing myself with meaningless shags. Every time I come inside a stranger's body, I recognize that sex never feels as good as it did with…someone else.

Maybe I perform the occasional internet search to look for anyone called Catriona MacTaggart. I don't want to see her. It's curiosity, that's all. By the time the seventh year has elapsed, I force myself to give up on my obsess—make that my casual habit of searching for women with a certain name. Torturing myself had become a longtime habit before I ever met Cat. Now that torture is well and truly over.

At least that's what I think—until fate intervenes.

I never believed in that rot, and I especially did not believe it after Catriona walked out of my life. But I can't deny the event that occurs now seems far too serendipitous for my taste. I'm now living in Montana and working at Thensmore University as a professor of archaeology and ancient history. I've settled in enough over the past two years that I built a house, the sort that is, admittedly, too bloody enormous for one person and rather gloomy, with its crimson walls and dark trim fashioned from Indian rosewood. The paintings in the entryway feature various deities from mythology. A large portrait of the Fates, the Greek goddesses, occupies the entryway wall. Maybe this house is depressing, but I don't care.

One day, some twat who's probably a student at Thensmore decides to steal a priceless object from my private collection. Whoever the twat was, he destroyed the lock on the front door and the one that secures my personal collection of objet d'art. The particular item the knob stole has…special meaning for me. I want it back.

So I ring someone I haven't spoken to in years and ask for help. The gent is a social worker, but he has connections at the Met in London. I assume he won't remember me, but he does—and he wants to help. I suppose he empathizes when I tell him what the object means to me, though I do that only out of desperation. What if I am desperate? It's a temporary condition.

My old mate rings me a few days later with the name of a person who might be able to help me. He's an army veteran and a former MI6 agent, fresh out of his tenure as a spy. If anyone can help me and keep it confidential, this is the man for the job. So says my old mate. He gives me a phone number for the bloke. When I ask for his name, I get a shock.

Logan MacTaggart.

I pay for Logan's flight from Scotland to Montana, and my right-hand man picks Logan up at the airport. I wait in my study while Reginald escorts the Scot through the house.

And I finally lay eyes on Logan, Catriona's cousin, the one she had worried about deeply when he was first deployed to Iraq. I rise and offer him my hand. "I'm Alex Thorne. Welcome to Moirai House."

Logan shakes my hand. "Tell me what you want me to do."

"I see you're not a fan of pleasantries."

"No. What do you want me to do?"

Sitting down again, I gesture for him to do the same. "Someone has nicked an item from my personal collection, and I want it back."

"Do ye have any idea who stole it?"

"No. But I suspect it was a student at Thensmore University. I work there."

"Hmm. Why did you contact me and not the police? Or a private investigator?"

I consider Logan for a moment, wondering if he was always this suspicious or if his time with MI6 changed him. Catriona had called him "a sweet boy," but the man sitting across me is not sweet or a boy, not anymore. I've changed too, so perhaps Logan and I share more in common than I thought. "A mate recommended you. That was all I needed to know. Will you take the job?"

"Aye, I'll do it. Do ye have a picture of the item?"

"Yes." I pull a photograph out of my desk drawer and offer it to him. "This is the item in question."

Logan holds the photo and studies it. His brows hike up. He lifts his gaze to me. "If this is a joke, I donnae appreciate a scunner wasting my time."

"This is not a joke, though I freely admit I am a bloody annoying prat."

His brows rise even higher. "Ye know what 'scunner' means?"

"Yes." How much should I confess? I need his help, so I must make a few concessions to satisfy him. "I learned that word from Catriona."

Logan stares at me without any discernible expression. "Catriona who?"

"MacTaggart. Your cousin." I shift in my seat as if I'm uncomfortable, but that's rubbish. Nothing unsettles me, which means there must be needles under my arse. "I knew Cat a long time ago. We, ah, lived together."

The Scot keeps staring at me. Just when I think he must have suffered an aneurysm, Logan erupts in laughter. "You're the British erse who broke her heart. Every time someone mentions you, she spits on the ground and curses in Gaelic."

Well, at least she hasn't forgotten about me. Not that I care either way.

"So, Logan," I say as if I don't give a stuff what his answer might be, "are you still willing to take the job?"

"Aye." He stands and sets the photograph on my desk. "Donnae need this."

"Don't you want to know how much I'll pay you?"

He shrugs. "We can discuss that later."

I suggest we have a drink, but he declines my offer. Logan also says no to dinner. The Scot examines the two crime scenes, then leaves.

Two days later, he returns with my precious treasure. The former spy strides into my study one evening and sets the package on my desk, wrapped in a brown paper sack. "Ye didnae mention the laddie is a bodybuilder and the star of the university wrestling team."

I point at his face. "He gave you a black eye?"

"That's right. You said this would be simple, but ye lied. No wonder Catriona hates you."

"I apologize, Logan. I had no idea who had stolen the item, so I couldn't have guessed the job would be such a bother." I unlock a drawer on my desk and bring out several bound stacks of hundred-dollar bills, then hand them to Logan. "Here. It's the fee I had planned on giving you plus a bit extra for the trouble."

Logan fans the bills with his thumb. His brows lift the slightest bit.

I unwrap the package and gaze at the object he had retrieved for me—an empty bottle of sparkling white grape juice that bears the lip print of Catriona MacTaggart.

Logan eyes the bottle. "The laddie must've drunk the contents."

"No. It was already empty."

This time when I invite him to dinner, he accepts. We have a good chat, and Logan shares a few stories from his time with MI6—the stories he can tell without committing treason. I'm sure he wants to know more about me and Cat, but I can't talk about that. So I share stories about the moronic things college students do.

A few days after I reclaimed my precious treasure, I realize I need to stop obsessing over the past. So I run my thumb over the bottle to erase the lip print, then I toss the thing into the rubbish bin. I'd gotten rid of the engagement ring years ago. Why cherish a ruddy bottle? Throwing out the last remnant of my relationship with Cat will cleanse me of her forever.

Yes, I excel at self-delusion.

Three years later, I ask for Logan's help again. I've gotten myself into a bit of a mess, a habit I seem to have developed lately. Logan comes to my rescue again, but this time he brings his new love interest, Serena Carpenter. They convince me to fly to Scotland with them and face up to my past, though even they don't know the whole truth about me. But they're right that I do need to confront my worst mistake.

Logan cheerfully informs me that Cat has devised nicknames for me over the years, and that she only ever refers to me by those names. The British Bastard. The Limey Louse. The Soulless Sassenach. Maybe I am a soulless Brit and a bastard. But it's time I stopped hiding from what I'd done to the only woman I ever loved.

I'm about to see Catriona.

Maybe I should buy a suit of armor.

Chapter Twenty

Catriona

I stand on the green behind Dùndubhan, the castle owned by my brother Rory. He hadn't owned a castle back when I became involved with that British Bastard. In the past few years, Dùndubhan has become a hub for MacTaggart family gatherings of all sorts, including shinty and Highland games. I now wait among a crowd of MacTaggarts, as well as the Americans that some of them have married, waiting for the Soulless Sassenach to walk onto the green.

I can't see what's happening, but I hear a chorus of murmurs that suggests Logan and Serena have emerged from the doorway in the castle wall that serves as the entrance to the walled garden. Alex must have followed them out, based on the murmuring around me. I can hear Rory's voice echoing off the walls, though I can't see him or make out his words. He sounds angry, though, and that suggests he's giving Alex a tongue lashing.

Good. The Limey Louse deserves it.

But I can't let my brothers fight my battle for me, so I push through the crowd. Everyone begins to move out of the way, opening a path for me, and even my brothers step aside. I stop a few yards away from Alex. The fire of fury erupts inside me as I skim my gaze over him from head to toe. Aye, he looks as good as ever—better even than he had the last time I saw him. But I donnae care how attractive and sexy he is. The British Bastard needs to pay for stealing my happiness.

Everyone on the green has fallen silent.

The fury rises even higher inside me, too hot and caustic to hold back.

"You bastard!" I scream as I barrel toward Alex.

Only his eyes move—to widen in shock, of course—and he just stands there as if he's waiting for me to assault him. I swing my fist back and slug him in the gut.

Alex gasps and doubles over, stumbling backward. But then he straightens and clears his throat as if he wants me to punch him again. Aye, I'll give him what he wants. I pull my arm back, preparing for another strike.

But Alex catches my fist in his hand.

Maybe I haven't behaved in the most adult manner, but Alex Thorne tore my heart out and didn't seem to care at all about what he'd done. We exchange a few words, and Alex acts like an arrogant erse who doesn't give a damn about anything or anyone. Then I drag him into the garden, slamming the door behind us. What happens next leaves me shaken and confused—because Alex does something I never could have anticipated.

He seems genuinely upset.

Our argument provokes a depth of emotion that stuns me. Not just my emotions. Alex's too. Does he care more than he lets on? Did our breakup all those years ago destroy him too? Long after I walk out the garden door, leaving Alex alone in there, I keep thinking about our encounter at Dùndubhan.

After that day, I see Alex often at family events like Logan and Serena's wedding, and my brother Aidan's birthday party. On every one of those occasions, I snap at Alex and berate him with the nicknames I invented long ago. Alex knows exactly how to provoke me into lashing out at him, and I'm beginning to think he wants me to do that. Maybe he feels guilty and letting me verbally assault him—and sometimes physically assault him—makes him feel like less of a *bod ceann*.

Since Alex lives in America, I don't see him every day. I don't even know where in America he lives.

After months of occasionally bumping into him, I get a surprise job offer from Thensmore University in Montana. It's a tenure-track position, and the pay is good. I need to shake up my life, so I accept the job. A month later, I arrive for my first day as a professor of archaeology and ancient history, and I meet a very nice woman called Lydia, who is in charge of the human resources office. I go there first to fill out paperwork and receive a brief introduction to the campus. But Lydia tells me something that sets my blood to boiling.

"We're so happy to have you here, Catriona," she says. "Alex Thorne's recommendation tipped the scales in your favor. He swears you're the smartest, most capable archaeologist he's ever known."

My fingers curl into my palms, as stiff as talons. "Alex recommended me?"

"Oh, yes. He gushed about you."

Though I want to grit my teeth and snarl, I force myself to stay calm. It's not Lydia's fault that Alex is a lying, conniving *bod ceann*. So I thank her for all her help and for letting me leave my bags in her office until I can pick them up after work. I had flown in early this morning and haven't even seen the house on campus that the university is providing for me.

As soon as the door to Lydia's office clicks shut behind me, I clench my fists and my teeth. Then I stalk through the building until I find Alex's office, thrust the door open, and march up to his desk. I stab a finger toward him. "Alex Thorne, you slimy, conniving bastard. What the bloody hell do you think you're doing?"

He gestures at his desktop. "Grading papers."

"Donnae be cute with me. How dare you interfere in my life."

Our argument goes on for several more minutes, but I get nothing from Alex except his favorite air of amused disinterest, as my cousin Logan calls it. He and Alex have become mates, but I've chosen not to criticize Logan for his lapse in judgment. My encounter with Alex leaves me feeling strangely invigorated. It doesn't help that age has made Alex even more appealing, almost irresistible. But I will never have a poke with him again. Never.

Still, I can't help wondering if his nonchalance is a cover for pain that he hides deep inside himself. His behavior nine months ago in the garden at Dùndubhan suggests I'm right about that. Maybe I shouldn't want to dig underneath Alex's skin and unearth the truth about him, but I need answers. Why did he push me away all those years ago? Why has he become so closed off? If I dig deep enough, will I find the passionate, sweet man I'd lived with for two years?

One way or another, I will find out. Our story isn't over yet. And Alex Thorne will not slither away from me again.

Get the full details of Alex and Cat's reunion in
***Lethal in a Kilt* (Hot Scots, Book Seven),**
then experience their own story in
***Irresistible in a Kilt* (Hot Scots, Book Eight).**

Love the

Hot Scots

series?

Visit
AnnaDurand.com

to subscribe to her newsletter
for updates on forthcoming books in the series
&
to receive free gifts for signing up!

Anna Durand is a bestselling, multi-award-winning author of contemporary and paranormal romance. Her books have earned bestseller status on every major retailer and wonderful reviews from readers around the world. But that's the boring spiel. Here are the really cool things you want to know about Anna!

Born on Lackland Air Force Base in Texas, Anna grew up moving here, there, and everywhere thanks to her dad's job as an instructor pilot. She's lived in Texas (twice), Mississippi, California (twice), Michigan (twice), and Alaska—and now Ohio.

As for her writing, Anna has always made up stories in her head, but she didn't write them down until her teen years. Those first awful books went into the trash can a few years later, though she learned a lot from those stories. Eventually, she would pen her first romance novel, the paranormal romance *Willpower*, and she's never looked back since.

Want even more details about Anna? Get access to her extended bio when you subscribe to her newsletter and download the free bonus ebook, *Hot Scots Confidential*. You'll also get hot deleted scenes, character interviews, fun facts, and more! Plus you'll receive audio bonus content narrated by Shane East, Vanessa Edwin, and Ava Lucas.

Visit AnnaDurand.com to sign up.